I'm Lavender
The Talking Book

Deborah Ann Hurt

11-17-05

Enjoy,

Deborah Ann Hurt

authorHOUSE™

1663 LIBERTY DRIVE, SUITE 200
BLOOMINGTON, INDIANA 47403
(800) 839-8640
WWW.AUTHORHOUSE.COM

First published by AuthorHouse 06/14/05

ISBN: 1-4208-0559-2 (sc)

Library of Congress Control Number: 2004098574

Printed in the United States of America
Bloomington, Indiana

This book is printed on acid-free paper.

Table of Contents

Acknowledgments

I want to thank my readers for their assistance and encouragement: especially Cecil Gilliland, Arlene Hurt, and Peggy Hiett. A special thank you goes out to Amy Mercer for her diligence and input. Also, I want to thank my husband, Glenn, for his many hours of help.

Dedication

In memory of

my parents,

Charles and Donna

Introduction

This book begins innocently enough with a bedtime story read by Dr. Robbins to his son and his son's friend. But the adventure and fun begin early the next morning when Dr. Robbins finds a secret about the old abandoned New England Book Factory across the street. A family of books must find a bonus book made in the factory that is still circulating or their home will be destroyed and they would have to go to a library.

In their search, they follow the story of a little book called *I'm Lavender.* Lavender and her book friends can walk and talk. They are mischievous in their first grade classroom. They have lots of fun and seem to always be in trouble. You never know what to expect from them or when they might be caught by the teacher. The funny jokes throughout the book and surprise twists make it fun reading for all ages.

But what about the New England Book Factory family of books that is looking for that bonus book? Will they find one that is still circulating within the twenty-four hour deadline or is their home doomed and they are destined to go to a library?

Chapter 1

A Bedtime Story

The night sky was dark as chocolate, and little Brown Bear was hiding out. He was near rocks inside a cave. It was his first night alone. His parents were attacked by a group of mountain lions and snatched away. It happened that afternoon on their way home from the water hole. He stayed awake most of the night.

When morning came, he got up early to make his way back to the water hole to fish. As he walked along, he thought about his parents and all the good things they taught him.

Suddenly, he heard a noise. When he turned around, he saw a group of tigers in a creek. They were coming toward him. They began to growl and hiss at him. He growled back, and then quickly turned around toward the water hole. He began to run. He ran faster than he had ever run before. He ran past bluffs and down a path all the way to the water hole. When he arrived, he was tired and frustrated.

The next day the same thing happened. That same day went on for weeks. Soon, the weeks turned into months, and before long, years had passed. He was grown now, and still the tigers were chasing him.

Day after day, for many years, it was always the same thing. They would growl, hiss, and chase. He would growl and run, but he never told another bear about his problem.

One day while the other bears were fishing at the water hole, Brown Bear decided to sit down on some logs nearby. As he sat, he began to think. *If only I had a helper, someone that would be kind to me and would listen. Then maybe together we could get rid of all these tigers.* As he thought, he heard a beautiful sound coming from one of the bushes behind him. When he turned around, he saw the prettiest red bird.

"What's wrong?" questioned the bird. "You look so upset."

"I am upset!" Brown Bear said. "I have been chased every day for years by tigers. I don't know what to do about it. I need someone kind to help me," he cried to the bird.

"If you look really hard, you will find a kind bear," the bird told him.

"Really? Are you sure?"

"I'm sure," replied the bird.

"When? Will it be long?"

"It won't be long at all," said the bird.

Brown Bear cried out one last time, "Please tell me how long. I must know, because I have been through so much."

"Okay," said the bird. "I will tell you this. Before your shoes wear out, you will find a kind bear." Then the bird flew away.

Brown Bear was very excited. *Could this be true? Before my shoes wear out, I will find a kind bear*, he thought. *I must begin looking right away.*

I will look for the oldest bear. The oldest bear will be kind and understanding. But the oldest bear was not kind. He only laughed and called Brown Bear crazy. *I know. I will go to the youngest bear*, Brown Bear thought. *Surely he will be kind.* But the youngest bear just laughed and called him crazy, too. Brown Bear was getting frustrated again. *I know.*

2

I am doing it all wrong. I will go to the one that is closest to my age. He will be kind and understand me for sure. But even the bear closest to his age only laughed and called him crazy.

Brown Bear didn't know what else to do. Every day, the tigers would growl, hiss, and then run after him

One day, Brown Bear stopped growling. He just ignored the tigers and ran. Besides, he was more interested in finding a kind bear.

Brown Bear looked to the tallest and the smallest. He looked to the loudest and the shyest. He looked to the fastest and the slowest. He looked to the strongest and the weakest. He looked to the happiest and the saddest. But they all just laughed and called him crazy.

One day, as he walked home, Brown Bear saw vultures dragging dead birds away from the creek.

"What's wrong with the birds?" Brown Bear asked the vultures.

"It is the creek. It's polluted. It's killing all the small animals. Soon, it will kill everything that drinks here," said the vultures. Brown Bear was concerned. *This is the place where I meet the tigers every day*, he thought.

The next day, on his way to fish, Brown Bear saw the tigers again. They were standing in their usual place, right in the middle of the creek. They began to growl and hiss. *You know*, thought Brown Bear, *as mean as they are to me, I still don't want them to die. I will tell them that the creek is polluted.* A little scared, Brown Bear walked toward the tigers. He told them all about the polluted creek. Then he turned and ran to the water hole. He ran so fast that his shoes were completely worn out when he got there. *My shoes are worn out*, he thought, *and I have not found a kind bear.*

The next day, on his way to the water hole, Brown Bear saw no tigers as he passed the creek. He stopped and looked around. Brown Bear knew his problem was solved, but he was still sad. *Red Bird told me that I would find a kind bear before my shoes wore out*, he thought. *Now my shoes have worn out, and my problem is solved, but I still have not found a kind bear.* Brown Bear didn't understand. *Why would Red Bird tell me that I was going to find a kind bear?* Brown Bear thought. "I will go back and try to find the red bird," said Brown Bear. So, he went back and sat down on the same log where he met Red Bird. Suddenly, the little red bird appeared with his beautiful music.

"Now, why are you upset?" asked the red bird. "Isn't your problem solved?"

"Yes, it is, but you promised I would find a kind bear before my shoes were worn out, but I didn't find a kind bear. Why didn't I? Why would you tell me that?" asked Brown Bear.

"But you *have* met someone kind," said Red Bird.

"Who?" asked Brown Bear.

"You! That kind bear lives right inside of you! You helped the tigers even though they were really mean to you. So, if you can't find what you need in others, look inside yourself, and you will find what you need every time," said Red Bird.

"Thanks, Red Bird. You're terrific," smiled Brown Bear.

The End

Chapter 2

Dr. Robbins and the Yellow-Tinted Sunglasses

After I finished reading the bedtime story to my son Matthew and his friend, I closed the storybook and placed it on the coffee table. Matthew was curled up at the end of the couch. He was born on August 27, 2000. His friend, David, celebrated my son's fifth birthday with him earlier this evening. He lives across the street and is a couple of years older than Matthew. He was resting in the family recliner. My wife Susan had gone upstairs before the reading of the bedtime story.

I stood up to stretch and looked at the boys. "Did you guys enjoy the little Brown Bear story?" I asked.

"I enjoyed it Dr. Robbins," said David.

Matthew nodded his head, and popped up. He turned toward the window and pointed to the clock that sat on the end table. "Dad, it's 9:15. It might be there!"

I looked down at my watch. "Yes, it might be."

David looked at Matthew, rather puzzled as he pulled himself forward and kicked back the recliner with his foot.

"What might be where? What are you talking about, Matthew?" asked David.

"Come with me and I'll show you!" shouted Matthew. He turned, ran up the steps and into the den. He walked slowly across the dark floor. When he saw the couch, he jumped on it. Matthew leaned forward against the back of it. He raised his hands and pulled back the curtains so he could see out the window.

It was a clear night. Matthew looked around at the stars, trying to spot the Big Dipper constellation.

"There it is, the Big Dipper," he shouted as I walked up behind him.

"Let me see," said David, stepping near the couch. David pushed his forehead against the glass and looked through the window. "I see it, too. I think I've seen it before. Dr. Robbins, can you see it every night?"

"Yes, if the neighbors don't have their porch lights on and it's not cloudy," I answered.

Then Matthew tugged on my shirt and said, "Let David look through our telescope, so he can see how the stars look through it." David looked over at me and then ran over to the telescope on the other side of the couch. Curiously, he gazed in it.

"Wow! The stars look pretty nice," he said.

"Dad, have you seen other pictures in the sky?" asked Matthew. He leaned against me and gave me a big hug. I looked down at my son.

"Yes, I have. I saw a woman once. She wore a hat and a dress."

"Did you see her through the telescope?" asked Matthew.

"No, we didn't have a telescope. I was just a boy. I was with your Uncle Jake on Grandpa's farm. We stayed out late that night running around on a hill next to the barn. We started gazing at the stars and that's when we saw her. I haven't seen her since."

6

"That's awesome, Dad. I would like to see her, too."

"Me, too," added David as he sat down on the couch and yawned.

"I'll tell you something else that's pretty awesome, Matthew. You start kindergarten class in the morning. I know I let you stay up past your bedtime, because it's your birthday and you wanted to see the stars. But from now on, since you're starting school, your bedtime will be 8:30. So, you need to tell David good night and get to bed."

David stood up and looked at Matthew and me. Matthew stood on the couch and frowned. "Okay, Dad. But may I ask you a few more questions?"

"What's that?" I asked.

Matthew replied, "Will they have books about the stars at school?"

"There might be a book in your classroom about the stars, but there will be plenty of other books--books about the alphabet, animals, numbers, and phonics. And there will be all kinds of colorful storybooks," I explained as I closed the curtains.

Matthew had a big grin on his face as he listened to me talk about school. "Dad, will my teacher let me bring my books home?"

I moved the telescope to the corner of the room as I continued talking to my son about school. "I bet your teacher lets you bring some of your books home. But, keep in mind they are not toys. You have to take good care of them so other children will be able to use them, too."

"How do we get books anyway, Dad?" asked Matthew, rubbing his hands across the back of the couch. David and Matthew watched as I walked near the couch and leaned against the wall.

"First, you get a good idea and proceed to write about it. The person that writes the book is called the author. When the author has finished writing the book, he gets a copyright so no one can steal his ideas. The book is checked for spelling and grammar, which is called editing. When that's done, it's published. That's where they put the pages together and give it a cover and a spine."

"Like the New England Book Factory across the street," interrupted Matthew.

"That's right," I continued. "Some authors want their book to be illustrated with pictures. When all that is done, the book is sent to stores to be sold."

David turned and started to walk out of the room. "I guess I'll go," he said. "Good night Dr. Robbins and thanks for inviting me to your birthday party, Matthew."

Matthew jumped off the couch. "You're welcome. Thanks for the dump truck," he said as he ran down the hall to his room.

David headed across the street to his house next to the old abandoned book factory. I watched David from inside the front door to make sure he made it home safely. As David entered his house, I saw a mouse run across my front steps. A little startled, I stepped back and knocked over my wife's favorite vase. It was a birthday present from her Dad. Luckily, I didn't break it. That would have made a mess, and I was glad I didn't have to explain it to Susan. *However, I'm going to remind her to stop feeding the dog outside. It leaves too many crumbs for the rodents*, I thought as I locked the front door.

I went upstairs to get ready for bed. When I opened the bedroom door, I was careful not to make too much noise, because Susan was already asleep. I quietly opened the window and pulled back the curtains. Then, I got into bed. As I lay in bed, I thought about Matthew and his first day of school. Soon, I was fast asleep.

It was a typical late August evening. The cool air circulated through the room from the open window. It wasn't long before the sun was rising over the old New England Book Factory.

Suddenly, there was a noise outside. It was so loud; it woke me. I sat up and looked toward the window.

It sounds like a three-ring circus going on outside, I thought. I got up to take a look. When I looked out, I couldn't believe what I saw. The New England Book Factory parking lot was full and people were going in and out of the building. The postman was putting mail in their mailbox.

I was amazed. I thought it seemed odd, because that factory had been closed for years. I wondered what could be going on. I decided to go over and take a look.

I put on my robe and house shoes and looked at Susan. She was still sleeping. I tiptoed out of the room and shut the door. I went downstairs and out the front door. I looked toward the book factory. The cars, the people, and the postman were gone. The old book factory was deserted once again.

I felt as though I was going to faint. I continued walking toward the book factory. When I was in front of the factory, I looked inside but saw nothing moving around. The entire place was covered in dust. All the equipment was outdated. The books on the shelves were covered in cobwebs, and part of the ceiling had fallen on the floor. A sign hanging on the bookshelves read, "Send these old books to the nearest library."

Suddenly, a man was standing beside me. I turned in surprise. My heart began to race. He was an old man with a full beard and a cane. He wasn't wearing any shoes.

"Can't see much if you look in like that," said the old man with a quiver in his voice. I took a step back.

"What do you mean?"

"I mean you can see a lot more if you look through these special glasses," said the old man. He pulled out a pair of yellow-tinted sunglasses and waved them in front of my face.

I took the glasses, put them on my face, and looked inside the factory again. At first, everything looked the same. But when I looked at the bookshelves, I saw books moving around on one shelf. The books had little arms and legs. They had faces on their front covers. One little gray book titled *Learn*

9

How to Publish was actually talking to another bigger book titled *Getting Your Book Assembled*.

They had their own little office right on the bookshelf. Computers, desks, chairs, and a picture of a bunch of little books were on the bookshelf. *Perhaps the picture is of a family and the bookshelf is their home*, I thought. It was hanging in one corner of the bookshelf. There was also a little door on the end of the bookshelf and a ladder that went from the top of the shelves to the bottom.

This is crazy, I thought. I quickly pulled off the sunglasses and turned to talk to the old man, but he was gone. I looked in all directions, hoping to find him, but he had vanished.

I put the glasses back on and pushed my face closer to the window. Next, I put my hand over my ear and cupped it against the glass window. My eyes strained as I watched the little books on the bookshelf.

The book titled *Getting Your Book Assembled* walked out the door and down the ladder to the floor. He walked to the front of the factory and picked up the mail that was delivered earlier. Then, he returned back to the fourth shelf of the bookshelf. He sat down on a chair and began to read the mail. The other book titled *Learn How to Publish* came over and sat on the edge of the desk. She was interested in what was in the mail.

From the look on his face, it seemed Assemble had read some rather disturbing news. I listened closely to the books' conversation.

Assemble said to Publish, "*The Book of Factory Records* sent us a letter. It says all the books that have been published in this book factory may be destroyed. However, any bonus books published were not checked. Unless we find a bonus book still circulating, they are going to close down our home. We have only twenty-four hours to reply before they send us to the nearest library!"

"We need to get the list of all the bonus books ever published in the factory as soon as possible. There *must* be a few bonus books from here somewhere, or at least one still circulating!"

"What's a bonus book?" asked Publish.

"When you order a certain number of books, you get one free. The free one is the bonus book," explained Assemble.

Assemble got on the phone and made a few calls. After a minute or so, two books from the top shelf made their way down the ladder to the fourth shelf. One was called Brother Edit and the other one was Sister Illustrate. Then, I saw one more book come running up the ladder from the bottom shelf. He barreled in the door ready to join the others. He was called Grandpa Copyright. A few more books joined them later.

Every book quickly grabbed a computer and began to search for a list of all bonus books ever published in the factory. They all worked really hard. *This task was not easy*, I thought to myself as I watched the little books from the window. But before long, Edit came up with a list. He got up and walked over to the door. Edit began to call out some of the bonus books that were published in the factory.

"There were bonus books published with the accounting, medical, and law books!" he exclaimed.

I could tell by the faces of the little books that they weren't happy with the list. They acted as though all those books had been destroyed; since they knew those kinds of books constantly change.

Finally, Grandpa Copyright found another list. "I had to use Sell's old computer. He was so organized."

"Our brother Sell's computer?" asked Illustrate.

"No, I'm sure it's our cousin Sell," added Edit.

"I don't think so," said Assemble.

"Then Sell who?" asked Publish.

"Sell Book, your uncle," replied Grandpa Copyright.

After listening to their conversation for a few minutes, I could tell that Sell was a pretty popular name in that factory. It seemed every book there was related to a Sell.

Then, Grandpa Copyright stood up and read his list. "Accounting, law, medical, children's--"

"Stop right there," interrupted Assemble. "Did you say children's books?"

"Yes, it says right here that we published one bonus book for a child forty years ago."

"Now you're talking!" said Assemble. "I really believe it could still be out there somewhere!"

"Maybe our home will be able to stay open after all," noted Publish.

"Get back on Uncle Sell's computer and find out the name of the book. We must follow the history of that book to see if it is still in circulation," instructed Assemble.

So, Grandpa Copyright got back on Uncle Sell's computer. He discovered the name of the book and where it had been sent. Edit and Illustrate gathered around and watched. Grandpa Copyright printed the information and handed it to Illustrate. She read it to the group of books, "The child's bonus book was sent to a private school called Apple Valley Elementary, in 1965. It was a first grade reader titled *I'm Lavender.*"

"Surely the little book is still around somewhere!" cried Publish.

Assemble went to the file drawer and pulled out an old film of Apple Valley Elementary dated 1965. He pulled down a screen from the top of the bookcase. Next, he loaded the film in a projector. The book family gathered around the screen to watch the history of the little reading book titled *I'm Lavender.*

I started watching the film from outside the window. I could see it very clearly now with the yellow-tinted sunglasses. Every book in the family was watching the film but one, and that was Uncle Sell. Somebody said he was away sightseeing and was unable to make it back. But when I looked in the back of the factory, I saw an old book propped in a window to keep it open. The name on it was *Selling Your Book. Could that be their Uncle Sell?* I wondered.

The film began in August, 1965. It started with a man entering the New England Book Factory. When he came inside, he walked up to the front counter. He was a handsome young man in his late twenties, dressed in a suit and tie.

The clerk heard the front bell ring. She approached the counter.

"May I help you?" she questioned the man.

"Yes, my name is Mr. Green. I'm the principal at Apple Valley Elementary School. I'm here to pick up ten children's books that were ordered this month by Mrs. Napps for her first grade class," he told the clerk. Then he handed the clerk the following list of books:

Dinosaurs of the Past
My Alphabet Book
My Little Book of Numbers
Observing Our World
Book of Tall Tales
The Phonics Book
Spelling is Fun
Learning How to Respect
Nursery Rhymes
and the bonus book
I'm Lavender

The clerk quickly found his order and placed the books in a box. Mr. Green paid for the books and headed to the school.

It was Friday, and the teachers were preparing their classrooms for the new school year which would start on Monday.

When Mr. Green arrived at the school, he carried the box of books to Mrs. Napps' classroom. She was in the back of the room, dusting the bookshelves, and noticed Mr. Green when he entered the room. He set the box of books on her desk.

"Is that my order from the New England Book Factory?" she asked him.

"It is."

"I can't wait to see these books!" she told him as she put down her dust cloth, pushed her black framed glasses up on her nose and smoothed her short black curly hair behind her ears. She weaved her slender body around several chairs and a desk as she hurried to the front of the class.

When she arrived, she sat down at her desk and pulled the box of books close to her then looked inside. "They are the cutest little books I've ever seen!" Mrs. Napps carefully picked up two of the little books. "Just look at these books: *My Alphabet Book* and *My Little Book of Numbers.* Aren't they charming!" she added.

"Yes, and I can tell there is something very special about these books, too...almost magical," he told her as he looked at them. He reached over and picked up the book called *Observing Our World.* "So, each book is different?"

"Yes, I thought it would be nice for each child to have a different book. Oh, would you look at this one!" Mrs. Napps said excitedly. She reached inside the box and picked up *Dinosaurs of the Past* and held it up. "I would have loved a book like this one when I was six!"

"It is adorable. Will you be leaving soon?" Mr. Green asked.

"Yes, as soon as I finish dusting and set these little books around the blackboard."

"Okay. Miss Spencer is still here, too, so before you leave the building, you need to talk to her. She has the key for the alarm. Here are the keys to the front door." He put the keys on the corner of her desk and walked out of the room.

After Mrs. Napps finished dusting, she put the four books that were removed from the box around the blackboard. She removed the last six books from the box. Three of them (*Book of Tall Tales*, *The Phonics Book*, and *Learning How to Respect)* were also placed around the blackboard. She left the other three on her desk. Then she went to talk to Miss Spencer. She found her in her classroom down the hall. Mrs. Napps walked in the room and said, "I want to show you the books I ordered from the New England Book Factory." Together they walked to Mrs. Napps' classroom.

When they entered her classroom, Miss Spencer immediately noticed the little books around the blackboard. "Oh, I love them. They are so sweet!" she squealed. She picked up a book on the blackboard tray and flipped through its pages. She put it back and walked over to Mrs. Napps' desk. "Are these books on your desk part of the order?"

"Yes, but I haven't decided how I want to arrange them yet," replied Mrs. Napps.

Miss Spencer noticed the book *I'm Lavender* on the desk and picked it up to show Mrs. Napps. "I like this one the best of the ten. It's really unique." She put it back on the desk.

Mrs. Napps walked over to her desk. She picked up the last three books (*Nursery Rhymes*, *Spelling is Fun* and *I'm Lavender)* and placed them around the blackboard with the other books. She stepped back and looked at her arrangement of the books. They looked nice to her. Miss Spencer could tell she was happy with the arrangement.

"Your room looks great. It looks like you're ready to start school on Monday," said Miss Spencer.

"I need to finish a bulletin board and remove a few old books on that bottom shelf in the back. I think I will do that first thing Monday morning," Mrs. Napps pointed out.

"I have a few more things to do, too," added Miss Spencer as she walked toward the door.

Mrs. Napps grabbed her purse and picked up the keys Mr. Green had left her. She went toward the light switch and turned off the lights. Both ladies walked out of the room, and Mrs. Napps locked her classroom door behind them.

Chapter 3

Exploring a Classroom

It was late in the afternoon, and Mrs. Napps' classroom was quiet now. Everything was in its place, waiting for Monday morning.

Suddenly, there was movement on the blackboard tray. The little book *I'm Lavender* (Lavender for short) started to move around. She was looking around the classroom and knew Mrs. Napps had left for the day. She jumped to the floor so she could check out her new surroundings.

She was cute, a little purple and lavender plaid book filled with stories and lovely pictures painted with bright colors. She was a tomboy and very curious, but was sweet and sensitive about everything.

"Come on, guys! What's the problem? You don't need to be scared; no one's here but us. Don't you fellows want to see your new classroom?" she spoke out to the other nine books that were still leaning against the blackboard. She shouted to the little book called *My Alphabet Book* and then she called out to *My Little Book of Numbers*. "Come on, Alphabet! Get down here! You too, Numbers!"

The two little books, Alphabet and Numbers, looked around the classroom. After a few minutes they also jumped down to the floor and began to walk around.

Alphabet was a blue book with yellow letters that formed an arch around his cover. He was very handsome and had a crush on *The Phonics Book*.

Numbers was a black book with big white digits scattered across his front. He was bold and smart enough to handle most situations. Alphabet and Numbers were Lavender's closest friends.

Soon, all ten books were down on the floor roaming the classroom. Lavender spotted a group of older books on a bottom shelf near the back. She walked over and introduced herself. "Hello, I'm Lavender. I'm from the New England Book Factory. What are your names?"

"Our names don't really matter. You guys are the new ones. All of us are on our way out," spoke one old book as he lay pouting and covered in dust.

"Yeah, we are so old, we're forgotten!" cried another.

"That's right," whimpered another one. "We haven't been read in years. We're just waiting for someone to pick us up and drop us in the big black barrel, and who knows what will happen to us then."

"What's the big black barrel?" asked Lavender.

"It's a barrel in Mr. Green's office that takes away all the old books that are to be destroyed or recycled," an old book said.

"That's terrible!" mourned Lavender.

"Yeah, it is terrible! We've seen many books tossed away and now it's our turn. One day it will be your turn," grieved the old book.

Lavender was sad. She was a new book with crisp pages and a bright cover. She didn't realize that one day her pages could be torn and her cover faded. She didn't want to think about such things as that, not today. All she wanted to think about was her new classroom, her friends, and her place among the children as a book called *I'm Lavender.*

Lavender stayed with the old books a few more minutes, hoping to comfort them. But she knew nothing she said was going to help.

When she finished talking with the old books, she headed to the front of the classroom. It wasn't long before she spotted a new group of books. This group was all red in color and looked fairly new, like her. They were on the teacher's desk.

Before Lavender could introduce herself, Alphabet blurted out, "So, what's it like to be part of Mrs. Napps' classroom?"

"It's pretty nice," said one red book proudly. "Last year we were used as the leading reader for the class. Our stories were also picked for the annual play. The entire school came to watch the children perform."

Lavender liked her new classroom and couldn't wait for the first day of school. She looked at the back of the classroom and noticed a brightly colored bulletin board. There was a little loft in the corner near it. The loft was filled with a whole library of books. She also noticed a box of animal books underneath Mrs. Napps' desk. There were activity books under the blackboard and a bunch of songbooks on a shelf near the windows. The songbooks were fidgeting.

Lavender walked over to take a look.

"What's wrong?" she asked the songbooks.

"It's the bookworms! We can't seem to get rid of them," wept an old songbook.

"Well, maybe your problem is over." Lavender yelled across the room to a little book called *Dinosaurs of the Past.* "Would you come over here?"

Dinosaur stomped across the room. The desk shook from the pounding of his feet on the wooden floor as he came over to them.

"Will you eat the worms that are on these songbooks?" Lavender asked. "They would really appreciate the help." Dinosaur climbed the drawer handles that were on a cabinet and stood on top of the shelf. He walked over to the songbooks and began to eat the worms.

"Burrrrrrp!" Dinosaur let out a big burp after eating some of the worms. "Yummy," he said. "These are the best worms I've ever eaten."

Suddenly, a voice rolled across the classroom. "Dinosaur, that was rude. You're supposed to say excuse me," said the little book titled *Learning How to Respect*.

"Oh yeah, excuse me, but I couldn't help it, they're so fat and juicy," blushed Dinosaur.

While Dinosaur continued eating, Lavender got an idea. She leaped off the shelf and walked over to Mrs. Napps' desk. She climbed on the desk and looked for the student roll book.

Numbers was already on the desk, counting paper clips that were in an orange plastic bowl. Lavender found the roll book and opened it. She turned the first page and saw a list of names printed out.

"Numbers," said Lavender. "How many names are on this page?"

Numbers walked to the student roll book and counted the names. "Ten," he replied.

"How many books came over from the New England Book Factory?"

"Ten again," he answered, wondering where Lavender was headed with all the questions.

"That means each child is going to get one of us for their very own!" Lavender said grinning at Numbers.

"Maybe so," said Numbers as he continued counting.

The little New England books had fun that weekend, exploring their new classroom. They were running everywhere, checking everything out.

Dinosaur checked every corner in the classroom, looking for more worms. Numbers counted everything that could be counted four or five times. *Spelling is Fun* got into a spelling bee with the older spelling books and lost the spelling match.

The Phonics Book got into a little trouble. She ran into a desk and hurt her front cover and started making vowel sounds.

"O!" she shouted as loud as she could.

Alphabet was reciting his letters using the flash cards which were over the blackboard, but he kept an eye on Phonics. *Learning How to Respect* was up in the loft with the library books. She was making sure all the books were standing up straight and had their titles facing the same direction. *Observing Our World* heard a noise in the hall. He was looking under the door to find out what it might be. *Book of Tall Tales* was on the reading table looking at Mrs. Napps' newspaper. He was a friendly fellow, but you couldn't always tell how true his stories were. *Nursery Rhymes* was resting and watching the others with Lavender from Mrs. Napps' filing cabinet.

"Hey, Rhymes," said Lavender. "Why is Tall Tales going through Mrs. Napps' newspaper? He's acting like he doesn't care about the classroom."

"Tall Tales told me before he became a book, he was a Daily Herald newspaper. I guess he's catching up on the gossip," replied Rhymes.

All the little books had a great time that weekend. But soon the weekend was over, and the little books had to get back to the blackboard tray. They had to stand up straight and be still once again, because they wanted to be ready for the children on Monday.

Chapter 4

Lavender Meets a New Friend

It was Monday, the first day of school. It was a typical August day, partly sunny skies and humid. Mrs. Napps was the first one to arrive at the classroom. She came early to dispose of the old books on the bottom back shelf and finish the bulletin board.

Lavender and her friends slept while she tossed the old books in the big black barrel and finished the bulletin board. When she finished those things, everything was done and her classroom looked nice.

When the little books woke up they were excited. They were leaning against the blackboard with perfect posture, waiting for the children to come in.

As the children arrived, Mrs. Napps greeted each one. A chunky little girl with blue eyes and long red braids arrived first.

"Good morning Bessie Mae," smiled Mrs. Napps.

Bessie Mae stood in front of Mrs. Napps and tried to shape a smile as she wrapped one arm around the neck of a stuffed white polar bear. Not long after Bessie Mae arrived, a slender little boy with thick dark hair hurried into the room.

"Good morning Mrs. Napps," said Bobby.

"Good morning Bobby," smiled Mrs. Napps again.

Bobby tossed his head back and began to giggle. Bobby was followed by another dark-headed boy wearing glasses named Billy. Before long all ten children were there.

As soon as the children were settled, Mrs. Napps called the roll and read them a story. Next, she had the children introduce themselves and asked them a few questions. Soon, it was time for lunch.

When lunch was over, Mrs. Napps introduced a game. She blindfolded the children, one at a time, and spun them around. Then, she pointed them in the direction of the blackboard to find a book. Not knowing what book they would pick, it surprised them when they lifted their blindfolds.

Quickly, Jimmy (a lanky boy with sandy-brown hair) picked *My Little Book of Numbers*, but Sally pressed her lips tightly together and twisted her curly blonde hair as she stood back and thought. After a minute or so, she also reached out and grabbed a book. Her blue eyes sparkled with delight when she pulled up the blindfold and saw the little book *Spelling is Fun*.

When it was Bessie Mae's turn to choose, she picked *Dinosaurs of the Past,* and Aaron snatched *I'm Lavender.* Jane took the longest to choose. She couldn't make up her mind and had to put her hand on every book left until she finally walked away with *Learning How to Respect.*

When the game was over, each child had a book. The children were excited about their new books and couldn't wait to take them home.

Mrs. Napps explained that the books could go home one night each week but must come back to school with them the next day. She also explained that the books were a special gift and if for any reason they were taken away, they may or may not be replaced.

When the day was over, the children gathered their things. They grabbed their new books and headed home.

Lavender felt wonderful. She was going home with a little boy named Aaron. He was the shortest child in the class with brown hair, green eyes, and a pudgy round face.

When Aaron got home, his Mother, Mrs. Daniels, was there to greet him. She gave her son a big hug and asked several questions. Aaron pulled *I'm Lavender* from his book bag and placed it on the kitchen counter.

"What's this?" asked his Mother.

"Oh, that's my new book. I get to bring it home once a week."

"How nice! We'll read some of it tonight."

Dr. Daniels, Aaron's Dad, was on his way home from his office. He pulled into the driveway as Mrs. Daniels was preparing dinner. Dr. Daniels couldn't wait to hear about Aaron's first day of school. He walked up the front steps and opened the door. Aaron heard him when he entered the house and ran to the front door to greet him.

"Dad," said Aaron. "I want to show you my new book!" He held up his little book, *I'm Lavender*, so his Dad could see it.

"That's nice, son," said Dr. Daniels. His Dad took the book and looked at a few pages. Then he handed it back to his son and began to ask him about his first day of school. Mrs. Daniels walked up and greeted her husband then returned to the kitchen to finish dinner.

Aaron went to the den with his new book and sat down while his Dad went upstairs to change clothes. When Dr. Daniels returned, he went with Aaron to the study to read his new book to him.

After a few minutes, Mrs. Daniels called them for dinner. Aaron jumped off his Dad's lap and headed for the door, taking his new book with him.

"Let's leave your book in the study while we eat."

"No!" insisted Aaron. "I want my book with me on the table while I eat!"

Dr. Daniels began to lecture his son about the importance of good behavior. After a little coaching, his Dad convinced him to leave the book in the study and go to the kitchen.

Lavender listened as they walked out of the room and down the hall, away from the study. When she heard them in the kitchen, she sat up and began to look around.

Lavender couldn't believe there were so many books in this room. There were shelves on every wall filled with them. *They are all older and well used*, she thought. Some were thick. Others were tall, but to Lavender, they all looked really important. "Hello," she yelled across the study. "Can anybody hear me?"

Suddenly, a voice thundered across the room from a middle shelf. The voice scared Lavender. "What's a little book like you doing in Dr. Daniels' study?"

Lavender looked down and saw a big maroon book staring at her. "I'm Lavender. I'm Aaron's new schoolbook. Who are you?"

The maroon book spoke up. "We are a family of books filled with health information. We all work hard to keep Dr. Daniels' family and friends healthy. My job is to teach folks about the eyes. The shelf below me gives information concerning the ears and nose. The one above me tells about the teeth and gums."

At that moment, another voice emerged from the back of the room. "Yeah, and I'm all about weight management. My job is to keep folks slim and trim."

Lavender turned around and saw a tall, slim book on Dr. Daniels' credenza. The book was lifting a stapler and using it as a barbell.

Lavender laughed. She was pretty excited about everything going on. She said, "Maybe I can be part of your study room someday, too."

All of a sudden, Lavender heard another voice from a shelf to the right of her. It was a big brown book.

"No, you're not going to be part of this room. You're just a schoolbook. You don't belong here. You belong at school," said the big brown book.

"Who are you?" asked Lavender.

"I'm a book that tells folks about their lungs. Did you know that the lungs--"

"I hear someone coming!" interrupted Lavender. She heard footsteps in the hallway. They came closer to the study. The books quickly got back in their places. About that time, the door opened. Aaron walked in and went to the desk. He picked up his little book, *I'm Lavender*, and left the room.

He headed to the den with his book. When he walked in, he saw his Mother and Dad. His Mother was sitting in a chair with her legs on the coffee table. She was reading the newspaper. His Dad was on the couch, intently focused on a television program.

Aaron ran over to his Mother. He looked up at her and whispered, "Will you read some of my book to me before I go to bed?"

"Sure," she replied and stood up. They walked to a quieter place in the house, away from the television. After reading a few pages of Aaron's book to him, Mom decided to go out for ice cream. Aaron put Lavender on the coffee table in the den before they left. When they returned, it was time for bed.

Before Lavender fell asleep that night, she stretched out across the coffee table and thought about her exciting day.

The next morning came quickly for Lavender. When she woke up, she was still on the coffee table. She listened to dishes banging and smelled something good coming from the kitchen.

After a few minutes, Aaron came into the den. He walked over to the coffee table and picked up his book. He dropped it into his book bag and headed out the door.

Lavender couldn't wait until after school to tell her book friends about the wonderful evening she had with Aaron. When Aaron arrived at school, he was instructed by Mrs.

Napps to put his book on a shelf under a window. Soon, all the little New England books were back together. They were all piled up on the same shelf under the window.

Lavender was still sleepy after her visit with the Daniels' family. So, when Mrs. Napps started class, Lavender decided it was time to relax and take a snooze. As class continued, Lavender slept on. But it wasn't long before the dismissal bell rang and woke her up.

Goodness, I must have been really tired. I slept the whole day, she said to herself, as she looked at the clock.

As soon as everyone left the classroom for the day, the little books stood up to stretch. Numbers looked at Lavender and wanted to know, "How was your visit with Aaron yesterday?"

Lavender grinned really big and said, "I had the best time. His family read some of my stories, and I met many new books. They treated me like a princess."

"That's great," said Numbers, "My visit didn't go that well. I was hardly read, but they did treat me well."

"I know what you mean," added Alphabet. "Sherry didn't read me much either."

"You guys think you had it bad? Listen to this. Somebody dropped me into their washing machine and my pages are still wet," said Observing as he opened up his book to show them his damp pages.

"Well, that's nothing! Just look at me!" said Dinosaur. "Bessie Mae left me on the front steps of her house all night. Her Mother found me this morning on their way to school." Dinosaur turned around and showed them his soiled back cover. Their mouths dropped open.

"Oooh!" said the little books in unison.

Lavender felt bad about Observing and Dinosaur. She was hoping her book friends had only good stories to tell this morning. *Maybe their next visits will be better*, she thought as she leaped from the shelf to play.

Chapter 5

An Unforgettable Battle

Two months had passed since the little books arrived at school. Lavender and her book friends had adjusted well to their new classroom and the children had taken their little books home weekly.

It was the day before Halloween and a little breezy outside but nice. Mrs. Napps was dismissing the children. Soon, as the last child left, she closed her student roll book and stood. She picked up her purse and a box of activity books and left the classroom.

Lavender listened as Mrs. Napps locked the door from the outside. The lock made a clicking sound when Mrs. Napps turned the key. Lavender now knew she had left.

Lavender wanted to find Numbers to confirm what Tall Tales had told her that morning about Alphabet. The story was that Alphabet had given Phonics a bookmark. She sat up and went to find Numbers, because he was not on the shelf with the other books. Tall Tales said that Numbers saw what happened. Lavender couldn't wait to ask Numbers about the bookmark.

She found Numbers on the reading table with a book called *The Book of Careers*. Jimmy had forgotten to put his book on the little shelf under the window before he left to go home.

"Hey, Numbers," said Lavender. "Did Alphabet really give Phonics a bookmark?"

"He sure did. I saw him do it."

Lavender gazed up at Numbers with a surprised look. "Well, tell me about the bookmark!" Lavender anxiously waited for Numbers to answer.

"It's a pretty nice bookmark. It says 'I love Phonics'," replied Numbers. Lavender smiled with joy about Phonics and Alphabet. Numbers continued, "I want to tell you something else. They're going on a date tonight. There's no doubt about it; he's definitely hooked on Phonics!" Lavender's mouth flew open with amazement.

"And I think I know where they're going for their date tonight!" shouted Lavender.

"Where would that be?" asked Numbers.

Lavender continued, "Tall Tales told me that a couple of our friends were going to get in the box of animal books and pull out a few, just for fun. I bet it's Alphabet and Phonics!"

Numbers looked concerned. "They can't do that! I think Alphabet has lost a few pages. Doesn't he realize if they pull out one book, the entire box of animal books will wake up! They'll be everywhere, and this place will be a zoo! We must stop them!"

They raced over to Mrs. Napps' desk and looked underneath. It was too late. Alphabet had pulled out the book of tigers and woke up the elephants. The elephants had a hard time moving around and woke up the lions. The lions woke up the monkeys, and the monkeys woke up the bears. The bears stepped on the mouse book and woke up the mice. Before long, the entire box of animal books was all over the classroom.

They were climbing over chairs and running under the desks. They were climbing the shelves and swinging from the coat racks. Animal books were running in the loft and down the blackboard tray. They were scaling the bulletin boards and falling in the sink. They were running everywhere, just like Numbers predicted.

Alphabet turned around and saw his other book friends standing close behind him. He tried to explain, but was speechless. He was simply terrified and couldn't recite a single letter. He tried several times, but nothing came out. Finally, when a mouse book ran up his spine, he managed to holler out a couple of letters. "O, G!" he screamed as loud as he could, removing a mouse from his front cover. Phonics was happy to know her new boyfriend was going to be okay.

Lavender was frightened and looked at Numbers. "How are we going to get all these animal books back in their box?" Numbers thought for a minute and came up with an idea.

"When I was on the reading table, I had a good conversation with *The Book of Careers*. He told me if we ever have a problem in the classroom to call on him and he would help us. Go to *The Book of Careers* and tell him you want a policeman."

Lavender ran over to the reading table and asked *The Book of Careers* for a policeman.

When the policeman arrived, he took a look around. His dark blue eyes bulged from their sockets as he swung his police whistle watching the animal books scamper around the room. He quickly arranged a meeting on top of Mrs. Napps' desk. Lavender and all her friends were present.

The policeman shouted out some instructions right away. "I want two teams - a desk team and a walnut team. The desk team will be on the floor. I want this team to push the desks toward the animal books so they will be hemmed in. At the same time, I want the walnut team to go out the window and climb the walnut tree. They are to pick the walnuts and throw them through the window at the animal books. Maybe, with both teams working together, we can knock down the animal books and get them back in their box."

Lavender knew she wanted to be part of the walnut team. She thought it would be fun to climb a tree and pick walnuts.

The little books paired off. Half got on the floor, and the other half went out the window.

The walnut team included Numbers, Spelling, Respect, Rhymes, and Lavender. The rest were on the desk team. Lavender and her team quickly climbed the tree. Each little book crawled out on a different branch. When they got comfortable, they began to pick the walnuts and throw them at the animal books. They had only knocked over a few books when Spelling's branch broke. She went down to the ground, ripping her front cover halfway off. She began to cry.

Lavender heard something whimpering and looked down. She saw Spelling lying on the ground. She knew Spelling was in trouble. She climbed down the tree and ran over to her.

"Spelling, are you okay? Can you spell anything?" Spelling didn't answer. She was hurt pretty badly. Lavender hollered up to Numbers who was still in the tree, throwing walnuts. "Spelling fell, and she's hurt pretty bad! What should I do?"

Numbers looked down and saw Spelling. "Go back to *The Book of Careers,* and this time get the doctor. He'll take care of Spelling," he said as he aimed a walnut at an animal book.

The doctor arrived with a huge needle and a satchel full of colored thread. He wanted to match Spelling's color exactly.

While Spelling was being stitched together, Lavender climbed back up the tree. Before she was settled, another branch broke. This time it was Nursery Rhymes. Lavender saw Rhymes fall. She fell, cover open, flat on her pages.

"Oh no! Not another one!" cried Lavender. Lavender climbed back down and ran to Rhymes. "Are you hurt? Can you say anything?"

Rhymes tried to push out a few words. "Jack fell down and broke his crown."

Lavender yelled up to Numbers again. "Rhymes fell and broke her crown. What do you want me to do?"

"Go back to *The Book of Careers,* and this time get a dentist. He'll know how to fix the crown."

Meanwhile, the floor team was getting tired, and there were animal books still running around. The policeman needed more help. He looked around the classroom for another way to attack the animal books. That's when he noticed a stack of papers and laid them across the floor. *Maybe the animal books will slide down when they step on these papers*, he thought to himself.

Finally, all the animal books were down. Lavender and her friends quickly dragged the books back to their box. Then they got busy and pulled the desks back in place. After that, they were tired and sat down.

Spelling and Rhymes were feeling better now, after the doctor and dentist had helped them. All the little books looked around the classroom. It was a mess. There were pieces of cracked walnut hulls everywhere and papers all over the floor.

"Do we have to clean up this mess tonight?" sobbed Tall Tales.

"Yeah, I don't want to clean it up either," added Dinosaur.

"And I'm way too tired to do any more work tonight," said Observing.

Numbers stood up to talk. "I say we clean up this mess in the morning, before Mrs. Napps arrives." All the little books thought that was a good idea, so they went to sleep right in the middle of the floor.

The next day, Lavender was awakened by a voice in the hall. She sat up and looked around. *Oh no, the mess! We forgot to clean up the mess*, she said to herself. Quickly, she looked for Numbers. "Get up!" she yelled as she shook him. When he woke up, he saw a frightened little face staring him in the eyes.

"We forgot to get up and clean!" cried Lavender. "And now it's too late! I heard a voice in the hall!"

Numbers gulped, "Oh, this is terrible."

"Do you think Mrs. Napps will blame this mess on us?" asked Lavender.

"I don't have a clue who, but I bet it won't be us," he said confidently.

"And why not?" asked Lavender.

"Because Mrs. Napps loves us and so do the children. I mean, just think about it. We entertain them, don't we?" Numbers added.

Suddenly, they heard the doorknob rattle. Lavender quickly got back to her spot on the shelf but kept her eyes slightly open as Mrs. Napps walked in. The expression on her face indicated to Lavender that she was pretty upset with the condition of the classroom.

Mrs. Napps walked over to the open windows and looked out. Then she got a broom and began to sweep the walnuts.

That's when Mr. Green, the principal, walked in. His eyes opened wide when he saw the mess. "Mrs. Napps, what happened to your classroom?"

Mrs. Napps walked over to him and tried to explain. "I forgot to close the windows before I left yesterday, and I saw some branches down outside. I guess a rather strong wind came up last night and whipped around the classroom. I will have it cleaned up in no time," she told him as she picked up the rest of the little books and put them on their special shelf under the window.

Lavender felt bad about the mess but was glad the animal books were put back in their box. She knew Alphabet wouldn't make that mistake again.

Chapter 6
It's Party Time

As soon as class began, Sherry (a little freckle-faced girl with strawberry-blonde hair) noticed her bookmark in Billy's book and blurted, "Mrs. Napps, Billy stole my bookmark! Tell him to give it back!"

Billy glanced down at Phonics and noticed a bookmark poking out above the pages. He lifted his eyebrows in surprise and looked up at Mrs. Napps. "I didn't take it!" he said.

Sherry pointed at the bookmark in Billy's book and said, "Then how did it get there?"

Billy shrugged and replied, "I don't know."

"Billy, just give the bookmark back to Sherry," demanded Mrs. Napps.

Alphabet gulped as he watched Billy give the bookmark back to Sherry. Phonics looked toward the little shelf at Alphabet and rolled her eyes.

It was Halloween and a cold front had moved in overnight.

Lavender felt a draft coming in under the windows. She lay shivering on her little shelf watching the leaves fall outside. Most of the trees had lost their leaves, but some of the trees still had their beautiful fall colors.

Mrs. Napps had been busy that morning, draping orange and black crepe paper around the classroom and carving the class pumpkin. She also had the children draw fall pictures to help decorate the classroom for their Halloween party.

While the children were busy drawing their fall pictures, Mrs. Napps pulled out a few boxes that were stacked in the coatroom. She wanted the children to do a measuring exercise before lunch. As she scooted the boxes across the floor, Sherry became distracted and turned around to watch them slide by. She caught Mrs. Napps' attention.

"Mrs. Napps, are you going to light the candle in the pumpkin?"

"I might light it during the party. Now turn around and work on your picture. I'll be collecting them in just a few minutes," replied Mrs. Napps as she hurried by with the boxes.

Lavender and her book friends also heard the loud noise of moving boxes and turned to watch. They continued watching as Mrs. Napps prepared the table for the exercise.

One box was filled with salt and the other with rice. She sat the boxes on a back table and went to get some different sized cups. Next, she called half of the students to the table. The other half stayed at their seats and worked on their pictures. The children enjoyed dipping the different sized cups into the rice and salt to see how much each cup would hold.

When they finished the measuring exercise, Mrs. Napps pushed the table against the back wall. As she walked back to her desk, she collected the pictures the children had drawn.

Lavender watched as she taped the pictures around the blackboard. When the pictures were taped she whispered to Alphabet, "Those pictures look kind of scary, don't they?"

Alphabet looked at the pictures. He was looking for his child Sherry's picture. It was taped at the end of the blackboard near Mrs. Napps' desk. Sherry had drawn a pumpkin and cut out the eyes. Lavender found Aaron's picture. It was at the other end of the blackboard. He had drawn a black cat.

The cat's tail extended from the page with the help of a little glue. A few children drew spiders, and there was a picture of children at a party bobbing for apples. But the spookiest picture of all was the skeleton. It was creepy looking. It was drawn with a black crayon and seemed to be smiling at them. It had a verse at the bottom that read:

Hello, I'm Mister Bones.
You can't keep me in this picture cage.
At night when the moon gets bright,
I like to go walking right off the page.
So, when you hear something crack in the night,
Don't be frightened, hold tight,
It's only my bones, prancing in the moonlight.

Lavender shuddered when she read the verse under the skeleton. "Alphabet, did you read what's below the skeleton? The verse scares me!" gasped Lavender.

"Yes, Lavender. I read it, and it's just a picture with a verse at the bottom. It can't really jump off the page," said Alphabet reassuringly.

"I'm not so sure about that. So tonight, if the moon comes out, I'll be watching the skeleton."

"Who drew it anyway?" asked Alphabet.

"Dinosaur's special friend, Bessie Mae," replied Lavender.

Lavender had a hard time with that skeleton. She was really scared of it. She felt like it might just jump off the page tonight and come after her. She was so worried. She exhausted Alphabet with it, and then she told Numbers about it. So Lavender, Alphabet, and Numbers decided that evening, if the moon came out, they would all three sit up and watch the skeleton.

As Lavender and her two friends Alphabet and Numbers were staring at the skeleton, Mrs. Napps read the children a story from Bobby's *Book of Tall Tales*.

When she was done with the story, Mr. Green showed up at the door with a package for Mrs. Napps. Lavender turned to watch Mrs. Napps. Mrs. Napps took the package and laid it on her desk. Soon after that, she instructed the children to wash their hands and line up for lunch while she talked to Mr. Green.

As Lavender looked at the package, she was sure she saw it move. When the children left for lunch, Lavender put the skeleton out of her mind for awhile. She wondered what might be in the package that Mr. Green gave to Mrs. Napps.

"Alphabet, go over and see what's in the package on Mrs. Napps' desk. I thought I saw it move!" instructed Lavender.

"No, I'm not going over there. They may come back any minute, and I'll get caught on Mrs. Napps' desk. We'll have to wait until later," replied Alphabet. The package remained a mystery the rest of the school day.

Later that day, after the children had their spelling test, Mr. Green showed up again. A lady and a little girl were with him this time. The lady and girl walked in and stood near Mrs. Napps' desk while Mr. Green brought in a desk and chair. Lavender knew she was a new student. Mrs. Napps introduced her to the class.

"Students," said Mrs. Napps. "This is Katie West. She is joining our class today. Katie moved here from Ohio. She is six and has a brother two years older who's in Miss Spencer's class. Let's make her feel welcome."

Mr. Green placed Katie's new desk between Cathy and Annie. Mrs. Napps watched Katie as she walked over and sat down. She could tell that Katie was settling in nicely when she saw the three girls giggling before the party began.

The children had a lot of fun at their Halloween party that afternoon. Mrs. Napps lit the pumpkin and allowed the children to wear their Halloween masks during the party. Several moms and one dad came to help. They played a game called Pin the Spider on the Web and had plenty of things to eat.

The food looked delicious. Cupcakes with orange-colored frosting topped with candy corn, chocolate ice cream, and fruit punch drinks were among the many selections. Lavender and her book friends enjoyed watching the children have fun.

When school was over that day, Lavender couldn't wait to go over and check out the mystery package. She jumped off her little shelf and ran over to Mrs. Napps' desk. She motioned for Alphabet and Numbers to come with her. They quickly hopped down from their shelf and ran after Lavender. The three of them opened the package together. It was another New England Factory Book called *Book of Opposites*.

Lavender was excited and so were Alphabet and Numbers. Lavender motioned to the other seven little books to come over and welcome the new little book. It wasn't long before all ten books were there.

Lavender introduced herself, and then she introduced Alphabet and Numbers. Before she could introduce Observing, he noticed something different about the book and yelled, "Look, he's taller and thicker than we are, and he's shiny, too. I guess that's why they call him Opposite." Lavender laughed at his joke.

"I bet you're going to be Katie's special book friend," said Phonics. "I'm Billy's book friend."

Opposite didn't answer. He stood next to Phonics looking around the room.

As soon as all the little books introduced themselves and shook hands with Opposite, Numbers came up with a great idea. "I say we throw him a party. We must welcome Opposite properly." Observing was so excited he stood up on Mrs. Napps' pencil holder to second the motion.

"Okay," said Numbers. "I guess it's party time. The floor is now open for some good suggestions."

Phonics stepped forward and suggested, "I know what would be fun. Everyone should take a drawing pad out of their special friend's desk and tilt it against a desk. It will make a great slide and we'll have lots of fun. And when we're done sliding, we can throw confetti on Opposite's covers as he walks around exploring the classroom."

"And where are we going to get the confetti?" Dinosaur wanted to know.

The little books looked around the classroom trying to find something that would substitute for confetti. All at once Numbers found a solution. "We don't need confetti; we can use the rice from Mrs. Napps' measuring exercise. The box of rice is on the table in the back of the classroom."

"Oh, that would be perfect!" added Tall Tales.

"No, I think we should sit in a circle and play Book, Book, Color Book, because that doesn't make a mess," commented Respect.

Numbers piped in, "There isn't going to be a mess. When the party's over, we'll get the custodian from *The Book of Careers* to come and clean our mess."

"I still don't think it's a good idea to mess up the classroom again, and I'm not going to be involved. You guys can do what you want. I'm going to bed!" said Respect as she shook her head sadly.

Lavender got a worried look on her face and commented, "Respect might have a good point. Maybe we shouldn't mess up the classroom again. It's not very respectful."

"That's true," said Nursery Rhymes. "Respect does make a lot of sense."

"Look, you guys. This place will be nice and clean before we go to bed tonight, and Mrs. Napps will never know we had a party. Trust me; you all worry way too much," Numbers said emphatically.

Finally, Numbers convinced Lavender and the other books that everything would be okay. The little books had decided to party. Each little book got a drawing pad from their special friend's desk and began to slide on it. They were having a blast.

When they had finished sliding, it was beginning to get dark. It was time for the big rice throw. Quickly, they ran to the back and filled their cups with rice. Last, they climbed onto the desks and counters. As Opposite walked by, they sprinkled rice on his head. He really felt proud to be part of the classroom.

When all the rice was thrown, Lavender and her book friends knew the party was over. They looked around the classroom. Rice was everywhere. "I'll go to *The Book of Careers* and get the custodian," Spelling eagerly said to the group.

All the little books were tired now. While Lavender and Numbers sat down and waited for Spelling to return with the custodian, their friends headed off to bed.

Opposite hurried back to Mrs. Napps' desk and crawled back in his package. He was exhausted, but happy. *Oh, my aching book. I feel like I've been dragged through a knot hole,* he said to himself as he stretched out in his package.

The other little books climbed back on their special shelf under the window and fell asleep. After a few minutes, Spelling returned. She was alone. Numbers and Lavender were surprised.

"Where's the custodian?" Numbers questioned Spelling.

"*The Book of Careers* is not here! Annie took it home for the night."

"How do you know?" asked Numbers.

"When I couldn't find the book, I looked at Mrs. Napps' checkout list. It was on the list."

Lavender looked worried. "So, how are we going to clean up this mess? The broom is way too big for us," said Lavender.

Numbers said, "I don't guess we are going to clean it up."

"Boy, we should have listened to Respect!" added Lavender. "What if Mrs. Napps blames this mess on us?"

"I don't think Mrs. Napps will blame it on us, but I am curious how she is going to explain this one to the children," said Numbers as he, Lavender, and Spelling walked back to their special little shelf under the window.

When Lavender returned to her little spot on the shelf, she noticed the bright moonlight coming through the window. She stayed awake and watched it. Lavender still remembered the verse below Bessie Mae's picture and wanted to make sure the skeleton stayed on its page.

Slowly, the moonlight moved across the pictures taped to the blackboard. It lit up a couple of pumpkin pictures. A few minutes later it fell on the skeleton. Lavender gulped and thought she saw the picture wiggle. She looked a little closer and determined it was wiggling. "Yaahhhhhh!" she hollered out. Her shrill yell woke up Numbers and Alphabet.

"Lavender, what's wrong?" panicked Numbers.

"It's the skeleton! It's wiggling! LOOK!" cried Lavender. The three of them watched the skeleton picture and after a few minutes, it wiggled again. They all saw it move this time.

Lavender shrieked again, "Did you guys see it move? I believe it's going to jump off the page and come after us! Numbers, what are we going to do?"

Numbers jumped off the shelf and walked over to the picture. It was still moving. He pushed a chair close to the blackboard and hopped on it. Quickly, he reached his hand out and touched the end of the picture and lifted it up. Frightened half to death, he jumped to the back of the chair.

"What is it?" yelled Lavender from across the room.

"It's a mouse!" shouted Numbers. "He's on the blackboard tray behind the picture."

"Hey, I'm not just a mouse. I'm Moptop," said the little mouse with wiry strands of silver bristles protruding from the top of his head. "I've been in this building for years, keeping the classrooms crumb free. Just ask the songbooks or red readers; they know me."

"Oh yeah! What are you doing behind this picture?" Numbers grilled Moptop. "Are you trying to scare us?"

"No, somebody had something sweet on their fingers when they drew the skeleton, and I'm trying to eat it." The little books let Moptop continue and went back to bed.

Early the next morning, Lavender woke up when she heard the classroom door open. It was Mr. Green, and he quickly tossed something on Mrs. Napps' desk from the doorway and left. Lavender stayed awake, and before long, Mrs. Napps arrived. She walked over to her desk, put her purse down, and continued over to the reading table. She felt something crunch under her feet. She looked down and saw drawing pads and rice all over the floor.

"Oh my goodness, what's all this stuff doing on the floor?" she mumbled. She started picking up the drawing pads. When she was almost finished, Miss Spencer walked in the classroom. She walked over to Mrs. Napps and saw the mess on the floor.

"Why is rice all over your floor?"

"I'm not really sure, but when I got here this morning, I noticed my door was unlocked. I must have forgotten to lock it yesterday when I left. So, I think when the sixth graders had their Halloween party last night, some of them wandered in to play a Halloween prank," replied Mrs. Napps.

Lavender felt really bad as she watched Mrs. Napps clean up the classroom. She knew Respect was right, and next time she was going to try and follow Respect's example.

Chapter 7

The Broken Bookend

Two weeks had passed since Halloween. Lavender and the other little books had gone home with the children yesterday afternoon and were on their way back to school this morning.

It was sunny outside, but the wind made it a rather chilly day. The Thanksgiving holiday was fast approaching. The children made turkey drawings that were already being displayed on the wall outside the classroom.

Mrs. Napps began the day with a spelling bee. It was the boys against the girls. Aaron and Jane had spelled all their words correctly so far. After awhile, the boys fell behind. Soon, they were so far behind that it was going to be impossible for them to catch up. But Lavender and her book friends enjoyed watching the children play the game.

After lunch, Mrs. Napps had the children write reports about the first Thanksgiving in addition to their regular class work. The children were to use Mrs. Napps' new encyclopedias. The books had been delivered a couple of days earlier. The shipment included twenty-six encyclopedias, a dictionary, and two plastic bookends.

Mrs. Napps set her new encyclopedias next to the little New England Books under the window. When the class was ready to start their Thanksgiving reports, Mrs. Napps was available to help each child.

Sally was the first child to do her report, followed by Aaron and then Bobby. When the children finished, the reports were read aloud and taped across the top of the blackboard. Lavender and the other little books enjoyed listening to the story of the Pilgrims and the Indians.

Right before the dismissal bell rang, Lavender fell asleep. She slept peacefully for many hours. She was awakened by a strange noise that rumbled across the classroom, causing even Moptop to run under the door.

The sound was coming from the right side of the shelf. She looked to the right and saw Mrs. Napps' new encyclopedias. They were a lot bigger and stronger than Lavender, and it looked like Encyclopedia T and Z were in a pretty serious discussion. Lavender watched but stayed back. She listened as the encyclopedias grumbled at each other.

"No!" yelled Encyclopedia Z in a really rough voice. "You can't have my place next to the bookend! This spot has been in the Z family forever, and you're not getting it now! Just because you were popular with the children today and helped them with their Thanksgiving reports doesn't mean you can have any spot you want. So, I'm going to tell you one more time to get yourself away from me and don't touch my cover!"

Encyclopedia T stood next to the bookend. He bellowed out, "I hope you're recycled to notebook paper one day!"

"Well, I hope you're recycled to a paper bag! Now, get away from me and back to your spot!" yelped Encyclopedia Z.

Z and T started shoving each other. Then Z shoved T into the plastic bookend knocking it off the shelf. T decided to return to his spot after that.

Lavender quickly jumped down and ran over to the bookend. It was cracked pretty badly. She hollered to Numbers, "Hey, did you hear those encyclopedias?"

Numbers was at the blackboard, reading Jimmy's Thanksgiving report when it happened. "Yes, I heard them. They sound so silly, don't they?" he said, walking toward the bookend.

Numbers began to mock them. "I wish you were a stamp. Well, I wish you were a sticker. I get sick of hearing such stupidity. I tell you what I wish. I wish they both were recycled to a check with my name on it for about two million dollars. Then I could go to any library or publishing house in the country and meet all kinds of interesting books and wouldn't have to listen to those encyclopedias," laughed Numbers.

Lavender giggled at Numbers as they stood over the cracked bookend. By the time Numbers had arrived, some of the other little books were there too.

"Do you think we can find someone in *The Book of Careers* to help us fix this bookend?" asked Lavender.

"Yeah, let's go get *The Book of Careers* and find someone to help us," said Numbers. Numbers and Lavender and a few of the others walked over to the reading table.

Lavender opened *The Book of Careers* and began to flip through the pages. She was looking for a suitable career book to fix the bookend when the book flipped to the structural engineering page.

"What about a structural engineer? Could a structural engineer fix the bookend?" Lavender questioned Numbers.

"No, we don't need a structural engineer. Those guys build huge buildings called skyscrapers. We just have a little plastic bookend to fix, so keep looking," replied Numbers as he lay across the reading table tapping his front cover.

Lavender flipped a few more pages, and this time she landed on the carpenter's page. "What about a carpenter? Would a carpenter be able to fix our bookend?"

"No, carpenters deal mostly with wood. Let me have the book; I'll find something." Numbers started flipping through the pages when he spotted a page called Jack of all Trades. "Now here's a fellow that might be able to help us." They asked the Jack of all Trades to come over and look at the broken bookend. He picked it up and examined it closely.

"Can you fix it so it looks new again?" Numbers questioned Jack.

Jack began to shake his head as he offered his best solutions. "I would remold it for you, but I don't have the matching mold, and if I glue it back together, it will leave a seam. I guess I can't make it look new again." Numbers thanked the Jack of all Trades and dismissed him. The little books began to feel disgusted. They sat down and stared at the broken bookend.

"How are we going to fix the bookend now?" asked Lavender.

Numbers hadn't given up, so he asked, "Does anybody have any other suggestions on how to repair the broken bookend?"

Tall Tales spoke up. "I know what to do. We'll open the door and leave it slightly ajar and open a few encyclopedias. Mrs. Napps will think someone entered her classroom, messed around, and broke the bookend. She'll never dream it was one of our kind that broke it."

Respect became agitated and interjected, "We can't do that, because it would be lying and lying is very bad. It could get us into more trouble. Besides, Mrs. Napps always keeps her door locked."

Tall Tales ran over to the door and wiggled the knob. "Yeah, she locked it," he said sheepishly.

"Respect's right. I don't think we should tell a lie about the bookend," added Lavender.

"I agree," said Dinosaur.

Lavender was getting worried. "So, what are we going to do about the bookend?"

Numbers walked over to the bookend. He picked it up and said, "I say we put it back where it goes. There's nothing we can do about it." He placed the bookend back where it was and headed to his shelf under the window. As he walked back, he tried to reassure the other little books. "Don't worry guys; everything will work out. It always does."

"Oh yeah, it works out until Mrs. Napps catches us," Lavender shot back at Numbers.

"Lavender, do you really think Mrs. Napps knows we walk and talk? I tell you she doesn't know. If she did know, she would lock us up," said Numbers.

Lavender had a hard time resting that weekend. She sat around worrying that Mrs. Napps was going to eventually find out that it was the books making all the messes. Finally, Sunday night after she watched Moptop make his rounds, she fell asleep. Lavender slept until the children entered the classroom Monday morning.

When the bell rang, Mrs. Napps stood and walked to the front of the class. She began to call the roll. Sherry had gotten up to get a drink of water, and before she was at the water fountain, she turned and looked toward the window. She saw the broken bookend. Her eyes opened in disbelief, as she walked a little closer. She paused to look at it for a moment.

Lavender couldn't believe someone found it so early. She was wondering how Mrs. Napps might explain it to the children.

Sherry interrupted the roll call. "Mrs. Napps, did you know one of your bookends is cracked?"

Mrs. Napps looked over at Sherry and at the window where the bookends were. "Really? Hmmm," she said as she began to walk toward them. "I looked at them Friday before I left, and I didn't notice a crack. And I was the first one here this morning. I wonder what happened!"

As Mrs. Napps approached, Sherry pointed to the crack in the bookend. Mrs. Napps picked it up and inspected it.

She looked out the window. "You know, Sherry, I believe I know what happened to this little bookend. I believe the heat from the sun came in through the window, heated the plastic, and cracked it. It probably wasn't made very well."

Lavender felt relieved again to be able to get out of another mess. She liked Mrs. Napps' explanation for the crack in the bookend. *If heat can really do that to plastic, I'm glad my covers are made of cardboard since my spot is under the window, too*, she thought to herself as she watched Mrs. Napps walk back to the front of the class.

Chapter 8

A Mysterious Little Book

It was three days before the Thanksgiving holiday, and the children were excited. The class coatroom was a busy place this morning and messy, too, because everything outside was wet. Another cold front had moved in during the night, bringing a lot of rain and blowing leaves around the school's yard.

Cathy had brought a special surprise for show-and-tell. It was a German schoolbook which belonged to her cousin Greta. Her family came all the way from Germany just to visit for the Thanksgiving holiday. The little book was titled *Wir Lernen Gegensatze* translated to English as *We Learn Opposites*.

Lavender was arriving late to class, because Aaron had a doctor's appointment. When Aaron walked in the classroom, the children were midway through reciting the Pledge of Allegiance to the flag. Aaron paused in the doorway until the children finished. Bobby was holding the flag at the front of the class.

When Lavender finally got back to her shelf under the window, she felt happy. Lavender had fun spending time with Aaron and his family. She glanced over at her other book friends, hoping to see more happy faces, but instead she sensed something was wrong. Numbers and Alphabet were prune-faced. Tall Tales and Observing looked sad, too. Dinosaur was almost in tears.

As soon as Lavender had a chance, she whispered to Alphabet, "What's going on? Why does everybody look so sad?"

Alphabet leaned toward Lavender and whispered, "Spelling is gone! Mrs. Napps said that Spelling kept Sally out of her seat too much, so she gave Spelling a ticket and sentenced her to the library."

Lavender was sad. "What! Tell me more!" exclaimed Lavender, forgetting she may be overheard by the children.

Alphabet's voice quivered as he went into more detail. "Sally was out of her seat again. This time, she was showing Spelling to Katie and Cathy when Mrs. Napps just took the book away. She put Spelling on her desk at first. Then, Mrs. Napps wrote out a ticket and taped it to Spelling's back cover, sentencing Spelling to the library."

"The library in the classroom?" questioned Lavender.

"No, she went to the big one down the hall! I bet we never see Spelling again. She looked so frightened when she left the classroom. That's a big place for such a little book like Spelling," Alphabet said with sadness.

"If only one of us could have gone with her; then it wouldn't be so bad," Lavender added much too loud again.

Suddenly Bobby stood and pointed toward the little shelf where the books lay. His face lit up as his mouth dropped open.

"Do you guys see what I see?" he blurted out.

Lavender shuddered. *Oh no, Bobby heard me talking,* she thought to herself as fear fell over her.

A second later, the classroom chairs began to scoot across the floor as the other students stood and looked toward the little shelf.

Lavender saw the children looking her way and panicked. *Maybe I should jump off the shelf and make a run for it,* she thought with a gasp. She gulped and shut her eyes.

Mrs. Napps hurried toward the window. "What is it?" she asked.

"It's a rainbow!" said Bobby.

The sun had popped out for a brief moment and made a beautiful rainbow across the sky. Lavender and her friends were relieved they weren't caught talking but were still sad about Spelling.

Lavender knew now why all her book friends were sad. She was sad, too. *I wish I could have said good-bye to Spelling. I'm really going to miss her because she was such a good friend,* thought Lavender.

It was a long day for Lavender and her friends, but the day continued with the usual routine; stories were read, lunch was served, games were played, and lessons were taught.

It was getting late, and the children hadn't spent as much time with their little books that day as they usually did. Therefore, Lavender couldn't wait for the bell to ring so she could stretch her legs.

Right before the bell rang, Observing noticed Mrs. Napps pulling something out of a little gray bag. *It looks like a new little book,* he thought. Watching her closely, he noticed her flipping through its pages. Then Bobby asked a question. It seemed he wanted a book on the back shelf.

Mrs. Napps got up and went to the back shelf, carrying her new book with her. She placed her book on the highest shelf in the back, and looked for the book Bobby wanted. That's when the bell rang, and the children were dismissed. Mrs. Napps forgot about her new little book she had placed on the top shelf. After she put a few things in their proper places, she got her purse and left for the day.

Observing wondered if anyone else noticed Mrs. Napps new book. He got up to talk to Lavender. "Lavender, did you see the new book Mrs. Napps put on the top back shelf?"

Lavender looked at Observing and said, "No, I didn't notice, but let's jump down and find out what it's called and its purpose in the classroom."

As they jumped from their shelf, Lavender motioned for Numbers to come and help. Rhymes saw Mrs. Napps put the book on the top shelf, also and came running over with Tall Tales and Opposite. Before they arrived at the bookcase, they passed Cathy's desk and heard her little cousin's German book of opposites humming. Lavender looked in the desk as she passed by and grinned at the little book, but Opposite stayed and talked. When the other books arrived at the bottom of the shelves in the back of the classroom, they tried to talk with the new little book on the top shelf.

"Hello there," yelled Lavender. "Can you hear me?" Lavender waited a few minutes for the little book to answer, but there was no answer. She tried again, "Hello there. What is your name?"

The little books heard a sweet, soft voice coming down from the top shelf. "Mary, George, Tony."

They looked at each other in surprise, and Lavender shouted up again. "What is your name again?"

"Sarah, Karen, Timmy," said the mysterious little book on the top shelf.

The little books began to laugh.

"Let me try this time," said Numbers. He stood as close as he could at the bottom of the bookcase and shouted. "Hello, I'm Numbers. What did you say your name is?"

"Joey, Tina, Sammy," the book spouted off more names.

"This little book sounds confused," said Tall Tales.

"It must be scared up there all by itself," Lavender added.

"Let's bring it down to us," insisted Rhymes.

Lavender looked to the top of the tall bookcase and said, "Who wants to go up and get it?"

"Not me," said Observing. "That climb is way too dangerous for me."

"Why don't we shake the bookcase so the little book will fall off?" Tall Tales piped in.

"No," said Rhymes. "Falling off a shelf could really hurt the little book. You remember what happened to Humpty Dumpty, don't you?"

"Yeah, I remember," Numbers joined in. "He broke into so many pieces; they couldn't put him back together again. I can't even count high enough to know the total number of pieces he was."

"I know what we'll do. Let's get *The Book of Careers* and get a fireman. He has a ladder and can bring the little book down safely."

Lavender ran over to Annie's desk and got the fireman from *The Book of Careers*. He came over with his ladder and climbed to the top shelf. He grabbed the little book and brought it down to them. The little books were surprised when they saw the new book.

"Look, you guys! It's a book of baby names! Do you know what this means? It probably means Mrs. Napps is going to have a baby, and she is using this book to help her choose a name. This book is not going to be a part of the classroom. It is Mrs. Napps' personal book," Numbers quickly said after seeing the book.

By the time the little books had the book of baby names returned to its place by the fireman, it was late at night. All but Lavender, Numbers, and Opposite had returned to their little shelf under the window and fallen asleep.

As Lavender and Numbers got settled on their little shelf for the night, Lavender glanced down and saw Opposite still on the floor. "Numbers, would you look over there at Opposite? He's still talking to the little German book of opposites. I think he likes her," said Lavender.

Numbers looked down at Opposite. "Yeah, I think he does too; just look at him laugh," smiled Numbers.

"How could he like her? They don't speak the same language," commented Lavender.

"Lavender, don't you know opposites attract! said Numbers.

By the time Opposite returned to their shelf, all the books in the classroom were in their place, except for *The Book of Careers*.

The Book of Careers decided it would sleep in the floor next to Annie's desk. It was used to the big reading table and felt cramped on a child's desk. That worried Lavender because she knew Mrs. Napps always checked her floors before she left each afternoon.

"Numbers," said Lavender. "What is Mrs. Napps going to think about *The Book of Careers* lying in the floor? Do you think she will blame us?"

"She won't blame us, Lavender," replied Numbers. "You should know by now Mrs. Napps has a special gift when it comes to covering for her sweet little books. Now, go to sleep and don't worry about it. She'll think of something."

As morning approached, the classroom looked good, except for *The Book of Careers* which was still in the floor next to Annie's desk. When Mrs. Napps walked in the classroom, she noticed the book in the floor right away. As she walked toward the book to pick it up, Lavender heard her whisper to herself, "The desk is tilted, and I guess it just slid off during the night."

Chapter 9

Planning a Rescue

It was the first week in December, and the weather was great. The temperature outside was in the low 70's. A front had moved in from the south causing warmer weather the whole week.

Today, the school was having a picnic; a little unusual for this time of year, but the faculty decided a couple of days ago to take advantage of the nice weather by having a picnic on the school grounds. They thought it would be a nice break for the children before winter.

Lavender was in her usual spot on the shelf under the window. She had just arrived at school with Aaron and was thinking about the wonderful time she had with him and his family over the weekend. She got to visit the study room again and be with all the big books. She also met some of Aaron's closest friends.

As she lay on the shelf, thinking about her visit, she heard a strange noise coming from Mrs. Napps' desk. It was a gruesome sound. Lavender looked toward the desk and was sure she heard something groaning. *It sounds like something's in trouble*, she thought.

Mrs. Napps was in the back of the room at the reading table when Lavender heard the noise. Lavender wanted to go over and check it out but knew she had to wait. She knew that the school had planned a morning assembly and decided to wait until the class left for the assembly to check it out.

When it was time for the assembly and everybody had left the room, Lavender quickly ran over to Alphabet and Numbers to explain the problem. The three of them jumped from the shelf and ran over to Mrs. Napps' desk. They stood on the floor next to the desk and listened for the noise. Suddenly, something groaned again.

Numbers stepped closer to the desk and said, "I think the noise is coming from Mrs. Napps' bottom desk drawer." He pushed a chair next to the bottom drawer and jumped on its seat. "Come on, guys! Get up here! Let's get this drawer open!"

The three of them got on the chair and pulled the drawer handle, but they couldn't get it to open.

"I think we need more help!" said Lavender.

Quickly, they called for Phonics and Observing, who were nearby, to come and help them. When all five of them pulled the handle together, the drawer popped open. The little books looked in and were horrified by what they saw. It was their friend, Dinosaur. He was hurt and looked terrible. His covers were missing. Something had torn them off, and he had several pages ripped away.

Lavender was in shock. "Wh-wh-what happened to you?" Lavender stammered as she looked down at Dinosaur.

Dinosaur whimpered as he told Lavender and her other book friends what had happened. "This weekend, when I went home with Bessie Mae, she dropped me in the driveway. Later, when the family went out, they backed over me with their car. It tore my covers off. I was in the driveway nearly the whole day before her mother found me. I'm just lucky she had Bessie Mae bring the rest of me back to school."

"When Bessie Mae gave me to Mrs. Napps, she put me in this bottom drawer. Next, I heard Mrs. Napps and Mr. Green talking. They seem to think it would be best if I went in the big black barrel with the other old books to be recycled or destroyed. After that, Mr. Green said that Miss Spencer would be using the big black barrel in a couple of days to clear out some of her old books. That probably means they will be coming after me in a couple of days, too."

"Well, we can't let that happen to you," said Alphabet.

"That's right," said Numbers. "We must hide you from the big black barrel by getting you out of the classroom."

Phonics thought for a minute and came up with a solution. "I know," she said. "The school is having a picnic today, and the children will want us to go out with them because they'll want to read stories after they eat. After that they'll want to play games. During the games, a few of us books will sneak back inside the school and get Dinosaur out of the drawer. Then, we'll take him outside to the gym and let the physical education manuals care for him until we return to get him. By that time, the big black barrel will be back in Mr. Green's office, empty of all the old books."

"That sounds like a good plan," said Lavender.

"I agree," added Numbers.

"So, who's going back in to get Dinosaur out of the drawer?" asked Phonics.

"I'll go back in," said Alphabet.

"I will, too," said Observing.

"Me too," added Lavender.

"Okay then," said Numbers. "As soon as the games begin, you guys need to sneak back into the school. You get Dinosaur out of the drawer as fast as you can and out of the building."

When the assembly was over, the children returned to class. They worked on their lessons until it was time for the picnic. Lavender and her friends slept until it was time for the children to line up at the door. The little books woke up as the children grabbed them from their shelf to go outside.

Mrs. Napps led the children out of the building to the back of the school where the picnic was held. The school grounds were covered with the smell of burgers cooking and the sound of children's laughter. Mrs. Napps guided the children to a picnic table next to an old oak tree. She placed her basket on the table and told the children to put their books next to the basket. As the children lined up to get their food, Mrs. Napps prepared the table.

Lavender and her friends were getting nervous as they thought about their big escape, going back inside the schoolhouse to rescue Dinosaur. They got even more anxious when the children finished their food and Mrs. Napps began story time. Lavender knew when Mrs. Napps started the next activity it would be time for her to sneak away. What if Mrs. Napps sees us sneak away? What would she do to us? Lavender trembled as she thought about all the things that could go wrong.

Suddenly, Lavender was startled. She felt something tap her on the front cover. She opened her eyes and looked around but didn't see anything. After a few moments, she felt it again, and then again. *Oh no*, she thought, *could word have gotten to Mrs. Napps that we are going to move Dinosaur?* She quickly whispered to Alphabet, "There's something tapping me; do you feel anything?"

Alphabet didn't feel anything, but Observing did.

"There's something tapping me, too," he said wondering what to do next.

That's it, thought Lavender. *Mrs. Napps heard our plan to move Dinosaur, and now she's trying to trick us.* Before Lavender could think another thought, she heard a blustering noise. All at once, Aaron's hand reached down and picked up Lavender, and the children started racing to the schoolhouse.

A pop-up thundershower was rolling in, and everyone was in a big rush to get inside. Phonics' plan to rescue Dinosaur had failed.

Once the children were inside, they had a hard time settling down. But, it wasn't long before the day ended and the children had gone home.

Lavender couldn't help thinking about poor Dinosaur. *If only we could do something else to help him. Maybe tomorrow we can try another rescue*, she thought.

Numbers walked over to Lavender and said, "Did you know Mrs. Napps is putting together a new book?"

"No kidding," said Lavender.

"Yes, it's on her desk. It's a book of paintings that the children did."

"That's neat," said Lavender. "I'm going to go over and see it." Lavender walked to Mrs. Napps' desk and looked around. "I don't see a book of paintings."

"It's on the other end of the desk, next to the flowerpot," yelled Numbers. "I'll come over and help you look."

Lavender waited for Numbers to come and help. When he arrived, he found the book of paintings right away. He grabbed the book and started to flip the pages. He was looking for his child's picture painting when he saw Aaron's picture painting.

"Oh, look at what Aaron painted. How nice! It's a picture of you, Lavender, and he wrote a little poem about you, too."

"Really!" said Lavender excitedly. She felt proud and couldn't wait to hear the poem.

As Numbers began to read the poem to Lavender, she relaxed against the flowerpot and listened.

Oh Lavender, Lavender, you're such a good friend.
You have taken me places
I've never been.
We've gone to the mountains,
And under the sea,
And deep in a jungle,

Just you and me.
I've learned so much,
Just being with you -
My colors and places
And how to read, too.
Oh Lavender, Lavender, you are a good friend,
I will love you forever, and that is the end.

The other little books listened as Numbers read the poem to Lavender. By the time he finished reading it, they all were on Mrs. Napps' desk, ready to look at the book of picture paintings. They wanted to see if anyone had mentioned them in a picture painting. As soon as Numbers put the book down, Observing picked it up. He started to flip through the pages when Tall Tales came up and tried to grab it from Observing. Observing pushed Tall Tales back, forcing him into Lavender. Then Lavender slid down, forcing the flowerpot off the desk.

"Oh no, not another mess!" cried Numbers.

Quickly, the little books jumped to the floor to look at Mrs. Napps' broken flowerpot.

Respect interjects, "The only book you guys need to read is my book. You can start with the chapter that teaches waiting your turn!"

"I agree," said Rhymes.

Lavender sighed and rolled her eyes at Numbers. "So, I guess we're not going to get blamed for this one, either."

The little books didn't know what to do about the mess. They really felt bad about it but figured Mrs. Napps would come up with a good explanation, leaving them off the hook again. So, they decided to get back on the little shelf under the window and leave the broken flowerpot in the floor.

As morning approached, Lavender was awakened by the sound of slamming car doors. She thought about the flowerpot lying in the floor but knew she had no control over the situation. She waited for Mrs. Napps to enter the room and got nervous when she saw the doorknob turn.

As the door cracked open, she heard a loud noise and a crash at the windows above her head. A rock went flying across the room. It landed right on Mrs. Napps' desk, where the flowerpot used to be, just seconds before Mrs. Napps entered the classroom. Mrs. Napps saw the mess. Mr. Green heard the noise and came running to Mrs. Napps' classroom.

"What's all the noise about?" he asked, looking at the mess that lay on the floor.

"Oh, the custodian, Mr. Drew, was moving the lawn mower to the shed for the winter and must have hit a rock on his way over to it," said Mrs. Napps.

"You mean he had his blade running!" noted Mr. Green.

"I asked him last week if he would cut the grass by the sidewalk when he moves the mower to the shed for the winter, and he told me he would," she added.

As they cleaned up the mess, Lavender was relieved, but she still wondered why Mrs. Napps could never catch on to who was really responsible for all the messes.

Chapter 10

Good-bye to Another Good Friend

By the time Mrs. Napps cleaned up the broken flowerpot, all the children but Bessie Mae had arrived at school. The books had a quick conversation. They decided to sleep during the morning activities but wanted to wake up by lunch to discuss another rescue plan for Dinosaur.

Right before lunch, Lavender was awakened by a piercing noise. She sneaked a look. It was Bessie Mae. She had just arrived at school, walked in, and slammed the classroom door behind her. She stood at the front of the class, holding her red sweater in one hand and a couple of books in the other. Before she sat down, she showed her books to Billy and Annie.

As the class was leaving for lunch, Lavender whispered to Alphabet, "Bessie Mae brought in two new books today. I'm going over to meet them. Would you like to come with me?" Alphabet was glad to go, and as soon as the class had gone, they headed toward Bessie Mae's desk.

Lavender arrived first. She looked in the desk and saw the two books. One was called *The Cat Monster*, and the other was *Goro, the Two-headed Dragon*.

She looked at them and tried to introduce herself. "Hello, I'm Lavender."

Goro reached out with his sharp claws and scratched Lavender on the nose. Quickly, she jumped back. With fire spewing from his mouths, he yelled, "Why do you want to wake me? Can't you see I'm resting! Now, go away!"

"Yeah," growled the Cat Monster. "We'll deal with you later!"

Lavender was terrified. She and Alphabet ran back to their shelf as fast as they could. When they arrived, the little books were in a meeting. They were discussing a new rescue plan for Dinosaur. Lavender ran up to Numbers and interrupted the meeting.

"Bessie Mae brought in two books today, and they *are* vicious! One is the Cat Monster, and the other one is Goro, a two-headed dragon."

Alphabet added, "The dragon scratched Lavender, and the Cat Monster threatened her! Look at the scratch on her nose!"

The little books looked at Lavender. Then they looked down at Bessie Mae's desk from the shelf and saw the two books lying inside. They didn't know what to think about the two new books. As the day continued, Lavender worried about them. Numbers was also a little concerned and had Observing watch them.

As soon as everyone had left for the day, the little books ran to Mrs. Napps' desk to visit Dinosaur. She had placed him in a bag and tied the end with a plastic cord. They opened up the bag and found pieces of other old books inside with him. They sat around and tried to comfort him. They even thought of several more rescue plans, but none seemed to work out.

When it was late, they put Dinosaur back in the bag and shut the drawer. They headed toward their shelf under the window. As the little books shut their eyes to fall asleep, they heard something growl below them on the floor. All of a sudden an awful voice floated up to their shelf.

"Where is Lavender?"

The little books were frightened and sat up. Alphabet knew right away that it was the Cat Monster and Goro. "Quickly," he whispered to Numbers. "We must hide Lavender."

Numbers looked around the shelf and saw a paper tray of weekly readers. "Quick!" he yelled. "Tell Lavender to get under the stack of weekly readers!"

Just as Lavender was settled under the weekly readers, the Cat Monster and Goro the dragon jumped onto the shelf. Their eyes glowed four shades of green as they marched across the shelf.

"Where is Lavender?" they demanded with a gruff voice.

The little books ran to the back of the shelf and defensively stood against the window as the Cat Monster and Goro lugged across the shelf.

Numbers spoke, "We haven't seen Lavender! I think she went home with a student!"

They didn't believe Numbers and continued their search for Lavender. They looked through the encyclopedias first. Next, they looked through the old songbooks. They continued to yell for Lavender. Lavender could hear their shrill voices from under the stack of weekly readers.

After they finished going through the old songbooks, they turned and noticed the stack of weekly readers in the paper tray. They walked toward the paper tray and started to go through the weekly readers when they heard a noise on the floor. It was Moptop making his nightly rounds. The Cat Monster and Goro looked down from the shelf but didn't see anything. In search of the noise, they leaped from the shelf.

As soon as they left, Numbers formed a plan and discussed it with the other books. "Why don't we get the bag that Dinosaur's in and put those two sorry pieces of walking cardboard in it? Then Mrs. Napps will put *them* in the big black barrel and not Dinosaur! We'll hide him under the songbooks on our shelf. I think if everybody works together, we can do it!"

Quickly, Alphabet and a few other little books ran to Mrs. Napps' bottom desk drawer. They pulled Dinosaur out of the bag and handed him to Opposite and Phonics. Alphabet returned to the shelf with the bag. He emptied the pieces of old books from the bag. Opposite and Phonics carried Dinosaur and hid him under the songbooks. Observing and Rhymes took the bag, stood on the shelf, and held the bag open. They waited quietly for the Cat Monster and Goro to walk by the shelf.

When they finally came around, the two books dropped the bag down on top of their heads. Numbers and Alphabet jumped from the shelf. They took the pieces of old books and threw them in the bag, hitting Goro in both heads and poking the Cat Monster in the eye. They tied the plastic cord around the bag, dragged it back to Mrs. Napps' desk, and put it in her bottom desk drawer.

Lavender was happy when she was able to crawl out from under the stack of weekly readers. The rest of the little books were also relieved when they finally had a chance to get some sleep. They piled up together on their little shelf, and just as they began to fall asleep, Lavender heard another noise.

She sat up and looked around the room. Lavender saw something coming toward her on the floor. She squealed to Numbers. "Look, the Cat Monster's out again, and he's headed this way!" Lavender grabbed Numbers and hid her face. Numbers was still as he watched the dark figure move closer.

"Lavender, that can't be the Cat Monster."

"Why can't it be?"

"Cause the cat's in the bag."

Lavender gasped, "If that dragon spews fire from his mouths, he'll make a hole in the bag and get out."

"No, he can't get out; the bag is flame retardant. It's printed on the side of the bag," reassured Numbers.

"I didn't see anything written on the bag," said Lavender.

"I didn't either. It was real fine print. Observing noticed it," said Numbers.

The dark figure climbed onto the shelf and walked right up to Numbers. It was a distinguished, older, brown book carrying an envelope. He greeted Numbers and handed him the envelope. Numbers took the envelope and opened it. He unfolded the paper inside and read it. "$2,500.00 due for services rendered from *The Book of Careers*." "What!" he screamed.

"Well, you didn't really think our services were free, did you?" goaded the old brown book.

Numbers gasped for breath. He was pretty upset. "Can't you see we're just a bunch of little school books? We don't have jobs or money. Would you give us a break?"

The old brown book asked a question. "Don't you know by now that there are two things that are certain in your life as a little book?"

"No, what are they?" asked Numbers.

"The big black barrel and a bill from *The Book of Careers*," he replied.

As soon as the old brown book left, the little books tried to settle down and go to sleep again. They decided to worry about paying their bill later.

The next morning, Lavender woke up when she heard chalk scraping across the blackboard. Mrs. Napps was writing some addition problems on the board. Lavender was still tired from all the excitement the night before. She was thinking about all that had happened and was glad most of the problems were solved. She looked at Numbers and Alphabet. They were still sleeping.

As soon as Mrs. Napps finished writing on the board, she started the reading groups. After that, she gave the children a spelling test. It wasn't until after Mrs. Napps collected the spelling test that Bessie Mae discovered her two books were missing. She looked and looked for them, but of course, she never found them.

Right before lunch, Mrs. Napps had some news for the children. One of the students was getting transferred out of the class, because her family was moving away. Lavender and her friends didn't pay much attention until Bessie Mae asked if she could have the transferring student's special New England Book, since her book, *Dinosaurs of the Past*, almost got destroyed.

"Numbers," whispered Lavender. "I wasn't paying attention. Who did Mrs. Napps say is getting transferred out of the class?"

Numbers shrugged. "I don't know. I wasn't paying attention either. I just hope it's not my child, Jimmy. I don't want Bessie Mae to get a hold of me, not after what happened to Dinosaur!"

"I hope it's not Aaron, either. I don't want Bessie Mae to get a hold of me!"

After lunch, Lavender quietly played a math game with Numbers. They played until they heard the big black barrel rolling down the hallway. Mrs. Napps was in the middle of a story from Annie's book, *Observing Our World*, when Mr. Green stopped the barrel in Mrs. Napps' doorway.

He looked at the class. Then he looked at Mrs. Napps and asked, "Do you have a book for me?"

She stopped her story and walked to her desk. She pulled open the bottom desk drawer and picked up the little bag that was tied with a plastic cord. She walked over and dropped it into the barrel. Lavender and her friends watched as Mr. Green pushed the barrel away from the doorway. They were relieved that the Cat Monster and Goro were gone and were glad they were able to rescue Dinosaur.

Before the school day ended, the children worked with Billy's book, *The Phonics Book*. After that, they performed a play in the classroom using the red readers. Right before the bell rang, Cathy sharpened her pencil at the sharpener next to the songbooks. She noticed a torn book underneath a songbook. She pulled it out and was surprised to see it was Bessie Mae's Dinosaur book.

"Mrs. Napps?" asked Cathy. "I thought you put the Dinosaur book in the barrel today!"

Mrs. Napps looked at the book and replied, "I thought I did, too. Here, let me have it. I'll take it home and give it to my nephew. He'll enjoy this little book, even if it doesn't have covers. I wonder which book was put in the big black barrel!"

Lavender and her friends were sad to see Dinosaur go, but they were happy he found a good home.

Chapter 11

A Student Gets Transferred

That evening, Numbers and Observing were on Mrs. Napps' desk inspecting a new book holder she received earlier that day. Numbers wanted to share his new find with Lavender. He looked toward the windows and spotted Lavender on the little shelf.

"Observing, would you look over there at Lavender?" asked Numbers.

"What for?" questioned Observing.

"Have you ever seen a cuter book?" Numbers nodded his head with a smirk on his face. "I'm so attracted to her purple plaids; she's one cool book."

"Numbers, I don't know what you're talking about. You can't know a book by its cover," Observing pointed out shaking his head.

"I know that, I believe her pages are just as cool," explained Numbers. Numbers wanted to tell Lavender he liked her, but he was too shy to tell her.

Lavender was resting on her shelf and thinking about Dinosaur when Numbers yelled to her from Mrs. Napps' desk. "Lavender, did you see Mrs. Napps' new book holder?"

"No, I didn't see it."

"It's pretty neat. Mrs. Napps doesn't have books in it yet. I think it came today. It will hold you up all by itself and leans you back in a resting position. You have to come over and take a look," he said as he jumped up on it.

"Okay, Numbers. I'll come and see it." Lavender turned around to talk with Alphabet who was behind her on the shelf. "I'm going to Mrs. Napps' desk; do you want to go with me?" she asked him.

"No, I'm going to stay here with Phonics," replied Alphabet.

"I'll come with you," said Opposite.

Tall Tales was listening and wanted to come also. "I'm coming, too," he added.

The three of them walked up to Mrs. Napps' new book holder and saw Numbers sitting in it. Lavender thought that it looked relaxing, too and slipped onto it also. A few seconds later they heard a voice right outside the classroom door. They looked toward the door.

"It sounds like Mrs. Napps and Miss Spencer!!" exclaimed Tall Tales. Lavender looked at the clock.

"It's 7:00 at night; they shouldn't be here!" she said. Cl–click, they heard a key enter the door lock.

"Quick, everybody hide!" yelled Numbers as he leaped between the dictionary and roll book on Mrs. Napps' desk. Lavender jumped underneath Mrs. Napps' desk calendar. Observing and Opposite hopped from the desk and crawled under Bobby's chair. Tall Tales was able to squeeze behind a picture on the desk.

What Lavender and her friends didn't know was that the school was holding a fundraiser dinner for the band in the school cafeteria that evening. Mrs. Napps forgot and left her ticket in the classroom.

Mrs. Napps ran in the room, followed by Miss Spencer and Mrs. Jones. "I hope the ticket is in the desk. Surely I didn't lose it," sputtered Mrs. Napps. She hurried to her chair and sat. She looked in the middle drawer. Her hands shuffled through the loose papers inside. "Here it is," she said as she pulled it from the drawer. "Okay, we can go to dinner now."

As Mrs. Napps stood, Mrs. Jones noticed a picture on the corner of her desk. "Who's the man in the picture?" Tall Tales heard the word picture and began to get nervous.

"That's my husband Tom," replied Mrs. Napps. Mrs. Jones picked up the picture to get a closer look. She grabbed it by the corner, swinging it in an upward motion. She didn't know that Tall Tales was stuck to the back of it. Tall Tales pushed hard against the frame. He tried to hold tight but almost lost his balance in the upward swing. Mrs. Jones put the picture down just as Tall Tales' foot slipped off the back of the frame and hit the desk. The ladies hurried out of the classroom and shut the door.

"Now that was a close call, and *that's the truth*!" gasped Tall Tales as he jumped out from behind the picture.

When Lavender crawled out from under the desk calendar, she was a little weary. She told the other books that she had done enough snooping for one night and was returning to her shelf to retire for the evening.

The next morning, Lavender was still thinking about the close call she had the night before. She also thought about Dinosaur and stared at his empty spot on the shelf. She still felt sad, but she began to feel better when she saw the children run around the classroom.

Mrs. Napps had planned a field trip for her class that day. They were going to the children's theater to see a play about jungle animals.

Mrs. Napps began class by writing animal facts on the board and gathering the animal books for reading groups. Bessie Mae even brought her new talking bear to school. It was a birthday gift, and before the reading groups began, she showed it to the class.

As soon as Bessie Mae sat down and put her bear away, the little books began to whisper. They decided that when the children left for the theater they would go over and have a talk with her Mr. Bear. They wanted to find out if Bessie was treating him nice, remembering how Dinosaur was torn to pieces.

Right before the children left on their trip, Mrs. Napps passed out the songbooks. They sang until Mr. Green showed up at the door to tell Mrs. Napps that the van was ready. The children were so excited. They quickly lined up and hurried out of the classroom.

When everyone was gone, Lavender and her friends paid a visit to Mr. Bear. They walked up and pulled the little bear from Bessie Mae's desk. Lavender shook his paw, and the little bear spoke up.

"Hello, I'm Patrick the panda bear."

"Hi, I'm Lavender and these are my friends. We were wondering if Bessie Mae treats you nice." They stared at the little bear for a minute, waiting for him to answer, but he didn't answer.

"Why doesn't the bear talk to us?" asked Lavender.

"I think the bear needs a little more attention. Why don't you shake his paw again?" queried Respect.

Lavender shook the bear's paw a second time, and immediately he spoke up again. "Hello, I'm Patrick the panda bear."

Lavender spoke to the bear again. "We were wondering if Bessie Mae treats you nice." But the little bear still didn't answer.

"I think he's ignoring us," said Rhymes.

"Yes, I think he knows a lot but doesn't want to say anything," said Numbers.

"So, he's just going to keep it all inside and tell us nothing," said Phonics.

"I say we be more respectful and leave him alone. He doesn't have to talk if he doesn't want to," added

Respect.

The little books didn't realize that the bear was programmed to talk when his paw was pushed, saying one line over and over.

Finally, the little books put the bear back in Bessie's desk and left him alone. Lavender was tired and thought she would go back to the shelf and take a nap. She slept until a lady walked in the classroom and sat down at Mrs. Napps' desk.

"Lavender, wake up," whispered Numbers. Lavender opened an eye and looked at Numbers. "Who's the lady at Mrs. Napps' desk?" he asked.

Lavender looked toward the desk. "I think she is the guidance counselor."

"I bet she's here to transfer the student," said Numbers.

"Oh dear, I hope it's not Aaron getting transferred. I don't want to go home with Bessie Mae," cried Lavender.

They watched the lady write out a note and put it on Mrs. Napps' desk. She walked toward the children's desks and stopped at Jane's. She cleaned it out and left the classroom. Lavender knew now that Respect's friend Jane had transferred. Respect didn't say anything, but she knew her new friend would be Bessie Mae.

When the children returned from their trip, Mrs. Napps called Bessie Mae to her desk. She handed her Jane's little book, *Learning How to Respect*. Right before the dismissal bell rang, Lavender heard Mrs. Napps tell Bessie to be sure and take good care of her new book.

Chapter 12

A Sticky Situation

It was cold and snow covered most of the school's yard. The jingle of bells woke Lavender this morning as Mrs. Napps entered the classroom. She had placed a Christmas wreath on the outside of her classroom door. Lavender enjoyed hearing the bells clink against the door as it opened.

It was only two weeks before Christmas, and the children had already started to decorate the classroom. The tree was placed near the front of the class, covered in tinsel and strings of popcorn. The only thing missing was the lights, and Bobby's mother was bringing them today.

Sally came through the door, reciting her lines for the Christmas pageant. She was excited that she had finally learned them. The class began practicing a week ago.

When the morning bell rang, Mrs. Napps spoke to the class about their mischievous behavior at the theater. It seemed the biggest problem was that the children wouldn't stay in line before or after the play. With that kind of behavior, Mrs. Napps had no choice but to enforce some strict rules. The rule was, if any child misbehaves in the next two days, their special little New England Book would be sold at the book fair on Saturday. That meant all the rules of the classroom had to be followed, or their books would be gone. Lavender and her friends listened as Mrs. Napps laid down the rules.

After Mrs. Napps lectured the class on their conduct, she had the children start on their morning board work. The children were quiet all morning and seemed to work harder than ever, because they loved their little books and didn't want to lose them at a book fair. Lavender and her friends watched the children work and were happy they were behaving.

Right before lunch, Sherry and Billy assisted Mrs. Napps as she changed the back bulletin board. They stapled up a winter scene with snowflakes and snowmen. It was completed with a blue and white border. When they finished, it looked good.

When the children walked in from lunch, Cathy saw a mouse run across the floor. "AAAAAAAAH a mouse! Get it out of here Mrs. Napps!" she screamed as she jumped in her seat.

Lavender knew it was Moptop. She snickered to herself as she watched the children hop around the classroom. As soon as the class settled down, they worked on their vowel sounds and took a spelling test. Soon after that, they had an art project. They made Santa hats and then went to recess.

Later that afternoon, before the children went home, Mrs. Napps called the class to the reading circle. She read them a few stories from Katie's book, *Book of Opposites*.

All the little books enjoyed the story, except Nursery Rhymes. She was lying back on the shelf and frowning. Lavender noticed her crinkled-up face and said, "What's wrong Nursery Rhymes?"

"Mrs. Napps reads every book in here but me. I never get read. She just ignores me," whimpered Nursery Rhymes.

Tall Tales heard their conversation and thought he would pipe in. "That's too bad, Rhymes. I guess everybody can't be as cool as I am. I don't have to go anywhere, and I get an audience. Just the other day, the library books were begging me to read to them, and the red readers were, too. So, I told them to be patient, and tomorrow night I would come and read some of my stories to them."

Suddenly, there was a clicking noise underneath the shelf. The sound got louder, and then a head popped out. It was Moptop. He looked around for Tall Tales but didn't see him. He whispered to the group of books instead, "Tell Tall Tales if he can get me some popcorn off the tree, I'll be glad to come and listen to his stories tomorrow night. I feel kind of bad for him, because I heard he's having a hard time finding someone to listen to him."

The little books tried hard not to laugh. They just turned toward Tall Tales and stared at him. He turned brighter than a red reader, and without saying a word, he shuffled off to the edge of the shelf. He knew they had figured out he was telling another big fat lie.

Before Mrs. Napps was through with the stories, the dismissal bell rang. The children quickly gathered their things and headed home, and the little books were happy everybody behaved.

Mrs. Napps wanted to stay late and finish up the costumes for the Christmas pageant. She asked Miss Spencer to come and help her. The little books lay quietly on their shelf and watched the ladies work for hours. As they were finishing, Miss Spencer walked to the window to look out. It was a bright night.

"It's pretty out tonight. I think it's a full moon."

"Oh, don't tell me it's another full moon. It seems every time we have a full moon strange things happen in this classroom."

"Really?" said Miss Spencer.

"Yes, really-everything in the room has been blamed for a mess, except the books of course. If something happens tonight, I'll just blame the books!" expressed Mrs. Napps.

"That's a good idea; I think you should," laughed Miss Spencer as they walked toward the door. Mrs. Napps turned around to look at her classroom one last time before leaving.

Everything looked nice, except a box filled with bottles of glue sitting on the corner of the shelf where the little books lay. It was left from the children's art project earlier that day, and she forgot to take the box back to the third grade teacher. She noticed the box but couldn't do anything about it that evening. She turned back around, walked out of the room, and locked the door.

As the ladies walked away from the door, the little books froze. They just stared at each other and gulped. Then Lavender broke the silence. "Numbers, you told me Mrs. Napps didn't know we walk and talk!"

"Well, I didn't know she knew! I mean, she just reads our stories and never talks to us. What's a book supposed to think?" asked Numbers.

"It's hard to know what to think. I guess she knew all the time it was us. She loved us so much she didn't want to say anything, but now we know even Mrs. Napps has a breaking point. So, if we make a mess tonight, I guess we'll be blamed," stated Lavender.

"I guess so," said Numbers. "But there won't be a mess tonight, because no one's going to move tonight. You guys got that? We are going to lay and rest until morning."

All the little books agreed that was the best idea. As the night passed, they lay on the shelf and watched the clock. Tick, tick, tick, the hours passed by slowly, but the little books were quiet and still.

After a while, Lavender heard a noise outside the window. She turned around to look out but didn't see anything. "My goodness, that's a loud car going by."

"That's not a car," said Phonics. "Believe me, I know my sounds. That's a helicopter. Can't you hear the swoosh, swoosh, swoosh?"

Then Tall Tales spoke up, "That's not a car or a helicopter. That's a train. You guys don't know anything!" He knew he had to get to the window to prove his point. So, he jumped over the box of glue bottles, catching his foot on its corner and knocking it to the floor.

The little books looked down. There was another mess in the floor. They couldn't believe it.

"So what do we do now?" asked Lavender.

"We go to *The Book of Careers* and get the custodian," replied Numbers.

"I'll go," Observing said, wanting to help.

The little books were happy they had *The Book of Careers* to help them. They sat down and waited for Observing to return, but when he came back he brought only bad news.

"*The Book of Careers* has been checked out again," he said, trying to catch his breath.

"No way!" exclaimed Numbers.

"Yes, I looked on the reading table and it wasn't there, so I looked on the check out list, and that's where I saw it."

"Who checked it out?" said Numbers.

"Jimmy," replied Observing.

Numbers looked at the books and said, "Okay, guys, we need to start cleaning the floor now if we're going to be finished by tomorrow."

The little books jumped to the floor and began to clean it. Alphabet and Phonics ran to the water fountain and snatched plenty of paper towels to use. They wiped the floor for hours, but the more they wiped, the more it smeared. When it began to get really late, the little books knew the glue wasn't going to come up. They stepped back and looked at the floor. It was a complete mess. There were bottles and dried glue all over the floor.

They knew they were in big trouble with Mrs. Napps. Lavender felt like crying. They went back to their shelf and sat. They were so worried. No one wanted to sleep. They just kept talking about the mess. Moptop overheard their conversation as he ran by.

"I'm so tired," said Rhymes.

"Well, if *The Book of Careers* wasn't checked out, this place would be clean by now and we would already be asleep," said Observing.

Moptop interrupted. "Are you guys looking for *The Book of Careers*?"

"Yeah!" the little books screamed.

"It's laying here in the coatroom, on the floor," he told them as he completed his nightly rounds and ran under the door.

"I guess when Jimmy put his coat on this afternoon to go home, he put the book down and forgot to pick it back up," said Numbers.

The little books were relieved and had the custodian from *The Book of Careers* come and clean up the mess before they went to sleep that night. When Mrs. Napps arrived in the morning, all she saw was a beautiful classroom and some sleepy little books, of course.

Chapter 13
The Book Fair

It was Friday morning, the day before the big book fair and the children's last day under Mrs. Napps' strict rules of good behavior. Lavender and her friends were hoping the children would follow the classroom rules one more day, because the books didn't want to wind up in the book fair. The book fair happens once a year, and hundreds of books are displayed and sold in the school's auditorium.

The school day started out with the normal routine of reading groups, writing from the board, and a spelling test. When the children finished their morning work, they had a few minutes left to sing Christmas songs before lunch.

Lavender and her friends relaxed and listened to the sounds of Christmas as they echoed across the room. Lavender's favorite song was "Frosty the Snowman", but Numbers enjoyed "Rudolph the Red Nose Reindeer" best.

The day was passing fast, but after lunch, a quarrel broke out. A couple of students got up to get a drink of water with Jimmy first in line. He pushed the handle on the water fountain a little too much. The water sprayed beyond the fountain and got Bobby's shirt wet. In surprise, Bobby jumped back.

"Jimmy, you got my shirt wet."

"Did not. I just wanted to get a drink," replied Jimmy.

All the little books were watching, except Numbers who was napping. The discussion between the two boys was beginning to get a little out of hand.

"Hey Numbers," said Tall Tales. "You better wake up!" Numbers opened his eyes and looked at Tall Tales.

"What's up?"

"Your number, that's what!" replied Tall Tales.

"Which one?" he asked. "My book goes to one hundred, you know."

"All of them!" replied Tall Tales. "Your child Jimmy just sprayed water on Bobby's shirt, and now Bobby's upset!"

Numbers watched the two boys. *Oh my,* he thought to himself. *This could be it for me.*

The boys ran to Mrs. Napps. She was putting the Christmas lights around the tree when Bobby interrupted her.

"Jimmy got my shirt wet!" He showed the teacher his wet shirt. Jimmy stood next to Bobby and tried to explain. The three of them talked it over for a few minutes; then Mrs. Napps decided to dismiss the whole matter.

The little books were overjoyed that the classroom rules were not broken. Numbers was especially happy, since it was his child Jimmy that was in question.

As the day continued, the children followed all the rules. There were math and language exercises before recess. When it was time for recess, Jimmy grabbed his book, *My Little Book of Numbers.* He was so happy it wasn't put in the book fair that he wanted to take it outside with him. Mrs. Napps granted him permission right before the children left. As soon as Numbers returned with Jimmy from recess and class resumed, Numbers whispered to the other books.

"The Cat Monster, I saw him!"

"Where?" asked Alphabet.

"In the bathroom! He's been recycled and is looking rather pale these days. In fact, I've seen ghosts that look better than him. Jimmy had to blow his nose, and he laid me on the sink. That's when I looked in the stall and saw him."

"What if he tries to come after me again?" cried Lavender.

"He can't. He's nothing like he used to be. He's just a white, thin, long strip of paper that's rolled up way too tight next to the commode. He couldn't possibly get away. He lives on a little roller thing that goes round and round all day long."

"Now that would make me dizzy," interrupted Alphabet.

"You mean he's nothing but a roll of toilet paper now!" whispered Tall Tales a little loud.

"Yes, he is, now keep your voice down," added Numbers as he looked around the room to see if anyone heard them talking.

"Wow, the expensive kind or the bargain brand?" asked Tall Tales.

"I don't know and don't care as long as he's out of here," added Numbers.

"You got that right," agreed Rhymes.

Numbers continued, "Anyway before I got back to the classroom, I saw Goro in the hallway. Somebody scorched and crushed him. He was turned into long sheets of bright colored flat paper stapled up to a bulletin board."

"I'm glad they got recycled. They won't be messing with us anymore," said Opposite.

"Oh guys, now that we're talking about recycling I need to tell you something," said Tall Tales.

"What?" questioned the little books.

"I heard Mr. Green and Mrs. Napps talking and they said that one day when my book wears out I would be recycled to popcorn boxes and used at the local theaters. Can you imagine smelling buttered popcorn all the time and watching movies all day long? And when my boxes are all used up, I'll just go back into the recycle bin to make more popcorn boxes. Boy, what a life! It's going to be great," said Tall Tales as he stretched across the little shelf.

"I wonder what I would be, if I were recycled. What would you guys want to be?" asked Lavender.

"I don't really want to be recycled. I just want to break out of here one day and see the world," said Observing.

"I don't want to be recycled either. I like being a book of respect, but it would be nice to have a powerful owner to spread my stories of manners and goodwill," said Respect.

"I wouldn't mind being another Numbers book but a much bigger one next time," said Numbers.

Before Numbers finished talking, the children started an art project. Mrs. Napps was passing out the materials for the children to make Christmas wreaths: strips of red and green tissue paper, paper plates with the middle cut out, and construction paper.

The children were busy much of the afternoon, crumpling and gluing the tissue paper to their paper plates when Sally's tissue paper began to get low. Thinking she dropped some, she looked around her desk. When she didn't find any on the floor, she stood and looked at Aaron's desk. He had stacks of it lying all over his desk. Without asking, she grabbed a hand full of his tissue paper.

"Sally, what are you doing? Give it back!" screamed Aaron. The shrill sound of his voice circled the classroom several times before it finally settled in Mrs. Napps' ears. She stood up and hurried to Aaron's desk.

"Why are you screaming? Aaron, you know better. You've just broken the first rule of the classroom."

"But Sally took my tissue paper," he cried.

"I'm sorry, Aaron. You know not to scream in class. If you have a problem, you bring it to me. I'm taking your book, *I'm Lavender*. It will be sold in the book fair tomorrow."

"Please may I have another chance?" he begged.

"No, you know the rules," she said as she turned and looked at Sally. She took Sally aside and started to talk with her when Lavender shut her eyes and began to cry. *I may never see Aaron again*, she thought to herself. Numbers and Alphabet tried to comfort Lavender.

"Don't feel bad. We'll all be gone one day, too. We're just paper and cardboard bound together with a little string, and nothing lasts forever," consoled Numbers.

"Yes, but Aaron was my friend. How could he let this happen to me?" asked Lavender as she dropped her head.

"I bet Aaron comes to the book fair tomorrow and buys you back," said Alphabet.

"I hope so. I was planning to live with Aaron when school was over this year. I don't really want to be with anybody else," Lavender cried.

Alphabet and Numbers stayed close to Lavender until the school day ended and they had to say good-bye. As soon as the bell rang, the children came to the shelf and got their book for the weekend. When all the books were taken away, Lavender remained alone on the little shelf. For the first time, she felt lonely. She watched Mrs. Napps gather a few things and stuff them in a bag.

Mrs. Napps walked over to the window and picked up Lavender from the shelf. She quickly crammed the little book in her satchel, shut off the lights, and left.

Lavender found herself pressed tight between two other books in the satchel in the dark. The little books inside shifted back and forth as she walked them to the auditorium.

When she arrived, she pulled Lavender and the other books from the bag and placed them on a table with hundreds of other books.

Lavender never saw so many different kinds of books. *The study room in Aaron's house doesn't have this many books*, she thought. Before Lavender could think anything else, Mrs. Napps put a big pink tag on Lavender's front cover. Then she walked away. All the little books were just like Lavender - restless, worried, and wearing big pink tags. It was a long evening. Lavender was scared. Not one book moved the whole night.

When morning arrived, Lavender felt a little better. She was hoping Aaron would be there soon to buy her. When the book fair began, people started to come into the auditorium. The place got noisy fast. People shuffled by the table where Lavender was placed. She saw many faces, but not Aaron's. There were books being picked up and sold all around her, but nobody seemed to notice Lavender.

Suddenly she heard a familiar voice and looked up. It was Bobby from Mrs. Napps' class. He looked around at all the books on Lavender's table, but again she was not noticed.

After a few minutes, Lavender heard another familiar voice. It was coming from the left side of the table. She looked toward the voice.

Oh no, it's Bessie Mae! I sure hope she doesn't see me, thought Lavender. Lavender shuddered as she watched Bessie come near.

Bessie looked all around at the different books on Lavender's table. Her eyes wandered right and left and then up and down, but Lavender went unnoticed again.

Bessie continued to look around, and as she was walking away she looked down one last time. That's when she let out a scream that rattled the windows.

"Daddy, I found the book I want! It's right here!" she reached down and picked up *I'm Lavender*.

"How much is it Bessie?" asked her Dad.

"It's two dollars," she said squeezing the little purple book.

"I don't know if you have that much money, Bessie," said her Dad as he helped her count her money.

Lavender listened as they counted each cent. She was hoping Bessie would come up short when she heard her Dad say, "Well Bessie, it looks like you have enough money after all."

Lavender was purchased and taken away that day. She was sad she had to go with Bessie Mae. As she was leaving the school, she began to think. *I bet Bessie brings me back to school on Monday. Then I'll be able to be with all my friends again and see Aaron, too. He'll buy me back. He'll buy me from Bessie Mae. I know he will. I just hope I don't wind up like Dinosaur before she gets me back to school.*

Later that afternoon, Aaron went to the book fair. He searched every table two and three times, but couldn't find his little book. Lavender was long gone, and Aaron was too late.

Chapter 14

Lavender and the Toy Shelf

When Bessie walked in the house, she went straight to the family room to get her jump rope. She laid Lavender next to the couch on the floor and went outside to play. Lavender lay on the floor and watched Bessie's parents move around the house.

After a while, someone pushed open the sliding glass door of the family room. It was Bessie. She walked in, followed by her dog Stacker. She put her jump rope down and walked right past Lavender into the kitchen.

Stacker, a two-month-old black and white collie, stayed in the family room, wagging his tail. His ears perked up as he scented something different in the room. He looked around and noticed Lavender next to the couch on the floor.

Lavender saw him, too and became frightened. She shut her eyes and lay still. Suddenly, she felt something licking her front cover. She opened her eyes to take a look. *Yuck!* thought Lavender. Stacker was right in her face. He began to growl and bark, "Grrr, woof, woof, woof!" He picked up Lavender with his teeth and dragged her around the room.

She felt terrible and wanted to scream but knew there was no one around to hear or help her. She felt the tight grip of his teeth as they penetrated through her covers. She was airborne one minute and crashing the next. *Yowl!* She screamed to herself as the dog dragged her out of the family room and down the hall.

Lavender heard someone approach. It was Bessie's Mother. "Oh you are the sweetest little puppy, and you're so playful today. Now give me the book."

Yeah, give her the book you mutt, and get your fangs out of my covers, thought Lavender. Bessie's Mom reached down, grabbed Lavender from the dog, and carried her to Bessie's bedroom. She put Lavender on the toy shelf and left the room.

If that's man's best friend, then I'm glad I'm a book, because I don't need a friend like that. That dog almost tore me to shreds. One minute more with him and I would be chopped literature, she said to herself as she looked down at the teeth marks that stretched across her front cover.

After a few minutes, Lavender began to feel better, until she sat up and looked around the room. As she looked around, she saw many disturbing things; a rocker full of dolls with missing heads, a dresser loaded with ripped stuffed animals, and many more books with their covers ripped off. *Oh my goodness, I'm in trouble now,* thought Lavender.

As she continued to look around, she heard someone call out her name. She turned around and saw Respect on the shelf above her. Lavender was so happy to see her friend.

"Lavender, what are you doing here?" asked Respect excitedly.

"I was sold in the book fair today to Bessie Mae. How are you doing?" asked Lavender.

"Fine," said Respect as she jumped down to Lavender's shelf.

"Do you think Bessie will take me back to school on Monday?" asked Lavender.

"I'm not sure, but I doubt it. She told her dolls earlier that I wouldn't be going back to school with her," replied Respect.

Lavender looked at the rocker of dolls with missing heads and gulped. "Does she ever read your stories or look at your pictures?" Lavender continued to question Respect.

"No, I usually just stay on this toy shelf and watch the family go in and out."

As they were talking, Stacker the dog wandered in the room. When Lavender saw the dog, she got a gruesome feeling. Quickly, she shut her eyes.

The dog came near and sniffed. Lavender could feel Stacker's wet nose and furry ears brush against her front cover. She was scared and wanted the dog to go away.

Finally, the dog turned toward Respect. Respect wasn't scared of Stacker. When the dog got too close for comfort, she opened her front cover and popped the dog in the nose. The dog whimpered and then he began to growl. "Grrr, grrr, grrr!" He snatched Respect from the shelf and carried her out of the room. Lavender heard Respect cry as she left the room.

Lavender was scared and wanted to go back to school. She lay on the toy shelf and waited for Respect to come back, but she never returned.

Later that night, when everyone went to sleep, Lavender crawled off the toy shelf. She went to look for Respect. She searched every room but didn't find her. As she climbed back on the toy shelf, a funny feeling ran down her spine. She was worried and confused and had a hard time getting to sleep.

The next day was Sunday. Lavender lay still most of the day on the toy shelf and watched the door of the bedroom. She was hoping someone would bring Respect back, but nobody did.

Every night for several days, as the family slept, Lavender crawled off the toy shelf to look for Respect but could never find her. Later, Lavender remained on the toy shelf for a few days without moving. She was frightened, lonely, and began to collect dust. She thought about the children at school,

Aaron, and the other books. She missed them and wondered what they were doing.

A few days before Christmas, Bessie was going shopping with her Mother, and she wanted to take Lavender with her. Lavender was so excited. She couldn't wait to get off the toy shelf, out of the house, and away from the dog.

Chapter 15

Lavender Goes Shopping

On the way to the shopping mall, Lavender saw Respect in the back seat of the car. After worrying so much, she was really happy to finally find her friend. They grinned at each other and wanted to talk but knew they couldn't, so Lavender sat back and wondered what a shopping trip would be like.

This was Lavender's first time in a shopping mall. As soon as they walked in, she got a strange feeling. She had never seen such a big place or so many people. It was scary looking to her. People were coming and going, and everyone was moving really fast. She was carried in one store and then another. There was so much stuff for a little book to see. Lavender thought about what she saw. She saw

Hats and mats and boxes of toys,
Shirts and pants that only fit boys,
Bags and tags and displays of ribbon,
Cats and dogs and fish all living,
Dresses and skirts and jewelry galore,
Tools and towels, knick-knacks and more,
Candy and cakes and bottles of drink,
And a store full of books to make you think.

Lavender had seen many things, and the day was passing fast. Everyone was cheerful, but tired. Later, Bessie and her Mom got stuck behind a long line of people, mostly children. Lavender couldn't imagine what the hold up was. After a few minutes of going nowhere, she managed to peek through the crowd of people and see the end of the line. There was a Christmas tree and a man dressed in a furry red suit sitting in a chair. As the line shortened, Lavender watched the children. They would go up one at a time and talk to the man in red and then leave.

When it was Bessie's turn, she walked up and put Lavender down beside the Christmas tree. When she was ready to leave, she ran to her Mother and forgot about Lavender.

Lavender saw Bessie as she walked away. *Oh no, Bessie, come back*, she thought. She wanted to scream. Lavender watched Bessie until she was completely out of sight. She didn't get nervous right away, because she figured Bessie would remember and come back. She waited and waited, and it was getting late. When the long lines of children ended and the man in red left, Lavender figured Bessie wasn't coming back.

Later, when the stores shut their doors and the mall became quiet and empty, Lavender began to get worried. She felt abandoned and panicked as she looked around. Many thoughts ran through her mind. *What was she going to do? Who was going to take care of her, and who was going to be her friend now?*

She stayed awake most of the night, crying. Suddenly, she heard a rustling noise coming out of the tree. She looked up and saw plastic angels dangling from the ends of its branches. The tree was filled with them. All of a sudden, an angel slid down a branch. It fell on a Christmas tag taped to a package close to Lavender. Lavender was surprised to see the angel.

"Are you okay?" she asked the angel.

The angel looked at Lavender a little oddly. "Am I okay? The question is, are you okay? I slid off the tree to comfort you, because I heard your cry. So what's wrong, and why are you here?"

Lavender was happy to see the angel and tried to explain. "My owner left me here, and now I have no place to go. I don't know where I am or how to get back. I'm lost. If my owner doesn't come after me, where will I go? I can't stay here."

"Well, I'm not sure. I've seen many wrapped boxes under this tree, but never a little book like you."

Lavender thought for a few seconds and then spoke to the angel. "I know; if my owner doesn't come back for me, I can be a gift. A book makes a really nice gift."

The angel looked at her with disappointment. "You're real cute and everything, but you're a little rough around the corners, and your pages are starting to wrinkle. I'm afraid you can't be one of our gifts. You have to be new."

Lavender was sad and looked down at her front cover. "That's terrible. I have no owner, and I can't even be a gift. So what's going to happen to me? When Christmas is over and they take the tree down, where will I go?" She looked up at the angel in despair.

"Don't worry; I'll take care of you. You're going to be all right," she reassured Lavender.

"You will? Are you sure?" Lavender was excited.

"Yes, I'm sure."

Lavender began to feel better. "I'm Lavender, what's your name?"

The angel smiled. "I represent someone different every year. This year, I represent Dana. She's a little girl who lives with her mother. She's seven and has brown hair and blue eyes. She loves to visit her grandmother, color, and eat pizza. Her favorite subject in school is math. She's a good student and is learning to ride a bike. A bike is what she wants for Christmas."

"So all the gifts here are for children," stated Lavender as she looked at the wrapped packages.

"That's right, all for children," she answered. "Now, will you tell me about yourself?"

"I'm from Apple Valley Elementary School. I'm a book in Mrs. Napps' first grade class. I have many other book friends. My special student is Aaron. I've gone home with him once a week since the school year began. He was good to me, and I had fun with him. He enjoyed all my stories. I really miss Aaron and my book friends. I would like to go back someday." Lavender felt better as she talked to the angel.

As the days passed, Lavender and the little angel stayed together under the tree and became good friends. The gifts kept piling up, until one day a couple of men walked up with boxes and began to collect them. Lavender watched the men as they gathered the packages.

"Hey, Joe," said one of the men. "What's the little book doing here? Are we supposed to take it, too?" he asked. Lavender heard the man and became frightened.

"Nope, we're instructed to take only the wrapped ones," said the other man.

When all the gifts were collected, Lavender and the angel lay under the tree alone. It was Christmas Eve, and the shopping center was packed with people. They were rushing everywhere. All day, Lavender and the angel watched children come and go. They also watched the shoppers as they walked by with their colorful packages.

When night came and the shopping mall closed, everything was quiet. Lavender looked at all the empty space and began to worry. She started to question the angel again. The angel was busy collecting small pine needles that fell under the tree.

"Now that Christmas is over, when will they come and take down the tree and put you and the other angel ornaments away?"

93

"Soon," replied the angel.

"And where will I go?" asked Lavender.

"You will come with us," the angel told her.

"What if they don't want to pack me, then what?" Lavender looked at the angel with wide eyes as she waited for an answer.

"I will make sure you get packed, too. Don't worry so much," she told Lavender as she continued collecting the small pine branches that were under the tree.

A few days passed since that crowded Christmas Eve, and the shopping mall wasn't as busy now. Lavender missed the hustle and bustle of the Christmas rush. As she watched the after-Christmas shoppers walk by, she began to think. *I wonder how the angel ornament is going to get me packed away, too.*

A few days later, Lavender woke up when she heard two men approach. She listened as the men counted the angel ornaments.

"Harry, I only counted forty-one angel ornaments. The list says there should be forty-two."

"Well, Randy, look around! Maybe one fell off the tree," replied Harry as he cleaned up the Santa area.

Randy looked under the tree and found the missing ornament. It was lying on top of Lavender. When he reached down to pick it up, he noticed it was stuck to a book. He tried to separate them but couldn't.

"Harry," he spoke. "I found the ornament, but it's stuck to a book. I can't pull them apart. I'm afraid if I try, then the ornament may break. Looks like tree sap got on the book, and the ornament got stuck to it when it fell."

"Then remove the name on the ornament so we can take it back to the office, and throw the book and the ornament in the box. We'll let someone else worry about separating them later. We don't have time to waste. We've got four more trees to pack away before lunch," said Harry. So the men pitched Lavender and the angel ornament in the box with the others and sealed it up.

Chapter 16

Lavender Returns to School

Every night when the shopping mall closed, the angel ornaments and Lavender crawled from the box. They wandered around the storage room, laughing, telling stories, and having fun.

Once a year, when the clerks came to get the ornaments from the box to decorate the Christmas tree, Lavender hid under the bottom flap. She did that year after year and was never caught.

Many years had passed since she met the angel ornaments, and she never forgot about Aaron, the school, or her old book friends. The shopping mall hadn't changed much after all the years. Apple Valley Elementary was still holding classes. Mrs. Napps had a baby and stopped teaching. Mr. Green moved to another state. Alphabet was able to find a good home with Sherry. Respect was taken by Bessie Mae on a trip to Washington D.C. and left on the steps of the Capitol. She was found by and taken home with a Senator. Observing came up missing from the classroom after a fire drill and was never found. Opposite was sent to another school. Numbers was dropped in the big black barrel by accident and recycled into a phone book.

Phonics got hung up under a shelf while running from Alphabet one evening. She couldn't get loose even after several attempts. She was found years later and sold to an antique shop. Nursery Rhymes went to a preschool and was read every day for years. Tall Tales was tossed in the big black barrel at a ripe old age. He was recycled into a box of paper mouse and rat traps and used at a local movie theater. Moptop left the school and moved across the street to a cafeteria.

The Book of Careers was still active in the first grade class. He became the official greeter for all the books in the classroom. In real life, the teacher used the book for a doorstop, but to the books he was a greeter and the best one ever. But Lavender was still hiding out in the ornament box with the angels.

One night, close to Christmas, while the angels and Lavender slept in their box, Lavender heard a strange noise. Seconds later, their box began to shake. Lavender and the angels bounced around inside. After a moment, all motion stopped, and everything was quiet again. Lavender thought someone came in the storage room looking for something, but she didn't hear any voices. A little confused, she listened a few more minutes and then went back to sleep.

The next morning when she woke up, she heard motors running and shouting voices. After awhile, a lady removed the lid of their box. Lavender was surprised when she felt the bright sunlight hit her front cover. She looked up and saw the blue sky. *We're outside*, she thought.

"What's going on?" Lavender asked one of the angel ornaments.

"There was a tornado last night, and it ripped the roof off the storage room." the angel ornament replied.

At that moment, a man spoke to the workers in the storage room.

"I just got word from the general manager, and he wants everything cleaned up and out of here by this afternoon. So keep moving!"

The lady that removed the lid reached in the ornament box and began to pull out the angels, when suddenly she saw Lavender.

"Hey, look what I found - a little antique book. Looks like a first-grade reader. What should I do with it?" she asked the lady next to her.

"I would say throw it away, but you better ask Henry since he's in charge."

When Henry walked up, one of the ladies handed him the book. "What should I do with this book? It was in the box with the angel ornaments."

He took the book and opened the front cover.

"This book belongs to Apple Valley Elementary. Isn't that right down the street?"

"Yes, I think it is," replied one of the ladies.

"Then send it back to the school and let them do whatever they want to with it."

Lavender was sent back that very day to her old school. When she arrived, the teacher put her on a new shelf in the classroom. She couldn't believe how everything had changed. All of her old book friends were gone. There were fifteen children in the class now and a new teacher named Mrs. Tess.

Lavender was placed on her new shelf and forgotten. Months passed, and no one disturbed her. When the new readers were stacked close to her, she couldn't believe how pretty and bright their covers looked since she had become so faded and dirty.

She watched the other books as they were picked up and read through the months. It made her think of Aaron. Lavender still remembered Aaron and how much he enjoyed her stories. She still missed him but knew he was a grown man now. *He probably has children of his own*, she thought to herself.

Lavender no longer worried about being thrown out or getting recycled. The big black barrel didn't even scare her anymore. She knew she wasn't useful and that her pages were torn and she was falling apart.

As winter turned into spring, another school year was coming to an end. One day, Mrs. Tess decided to do some spring cleaning. She wanted to clear out all the old books in the classroom. Lavender knew she would be on that list.

That afternoon when the children went out for recess, Mrs. Tess went to Mr. Waters' (the principal's) office to get the big black barrel. A few minutes later she went next door and asked the librarian, Miss Shaw, to help her.

When they started pulling the books and throwing them in the barrel, Lavender knew her turn could be next. As she waited to be pulled from the shelf, she looked around the classroom one last time. She remembered her old spot under the window and all her book friends. She remembered Aaron and where he used to sit. She thought about Mrs. Napps, the children, and all the messes her and her book friends had made.

All of a sudden, Mrs. Tess stopped working and looked at the bookshelves. "Miss Shaw, I think I need your step ladder to get to that top shelf." Miss Shaw dropped a few more books into the barrel before she left the room to get her ladder.

Lavender's face lightened because she knew she had a few more minutes to enjoy the classroom. Several minutes passed before Miss Shaw returned. When she finally returned, she set the ladder next to the bookshelves.

Mrs. Tess was eager to get the old books out of the room before the children returned from recess. She hurried up the ladder and missed a step. She lost her balance and fell to the floor, twisting her ankle. She was unable to move her foot.

"Mrs. Tess, are you okay?" Miss Shaw said as she looked down in surprise. "I'll go get the principal. Would you like me to call the doctor for you, too?"

"Yes, please do," replied Mrs. Tess.

When the doctor arrived, Mrs. Tess' ankle had begun to swell. After he examined her ankle, he was unsure if she had a break and would need it x-rayed. Miss Shaw went with her to the emergency room while Mr. Waters and the doctor stayed in the classroom and waited for the children to return from recess. Mr. Waters looked outside and saw the children lining up to come in. He looked at the doctor.

"I have a meeting with the fifth and sixth grade teachers at two o'clock about the school carnival on Saturday. I wonder if you would mind staying here for a few minutes while I go find someone to watch the class."

The doctor smiled. "Why don't you let me stay for the rest of the school day, since I don't have any more appointments today? I know a few math games the children would enjoy playing."

"Oh, that's wonderful. I'll let you do that," said Mr. Waters as he opened the door to let the children come in.

While the children took their seats, the doctor looked toward the back of the class and asked, "Can you tell me why Mrs. Tess was using the ladder?"

Mr. Waters explained. "Yes, she was throwing out all the old books on the back shelves."

"I'll throw them away if that's okay with you," said the doctor.

"That's fine with me. Just throw them in that big black barrel back there," added Mr. Waters.

The children played math games until the bell rang. After the children left for the day, the doctor walked to the back of the class toward the bookshelves. He grabbed a stack of books. He flipped one book after another into the barrel. It wasn't long before he grabbed the stack that included Lavender. As he started to flip that stack into the barrel,

Lavender was pulled first and quickly slung from his hand into the barrel. She felt herself falling and then boom. She heard a horrible echo as she hit the bottom.

Lavender was sad when she looked up from the bottom of the big black barrel. The books continued to fall in. After a few minutes, she could no longer see out of the barrel and felt squeezed as the books accumulated on top of her. When the barrel began to move out of the classroom, Lavender listened as the wheels clanked along the floor. She had little hope now, because she knew her end could be near.

Mr. Waters was in his office when he heard the barrel rolling toward the front door. He hurried out. "Let me help you," he said as he pushed on the double door. "I'll go with you and bring the barrel back."

The doctor rolled the barrel outside and then pushed it to the dumpster. Mr. Waters followed him there. The doctor picked up the barrel and tilted it toward the dumpster. As the books slid out, the doctor noticed a purple book slide by. He took a second look. "Oh I don't believe this!" the doctor said in surprise.

"What is it?" asked Mr. Waters.

"I think I just found my first reader." He reached in and pulled out the little book, *I'm Lavender*. He opened the back cover and read: Aaron Daniels, age 6.

Dr. Daniels was elated. "I truly can't believe this! After all these years, my book is still here. I'm going to keep it and put it on my desk at work. I can't wait to read it again," he said to Mr. Waters as he began to walk to his car.

Lavender was ecstatic and couldn't believe Aaron had found her. She was saved from the big black barrel. *It's great to be together again with my buddy Aaron*, she thought as he held her.

Even though Lavender's covers were old and faded and her pages wrinkled and torn, Dr. Daniels still saw her the same way he saw her when he was six - bright, crisp, and full of adventure.

As Dr. Daniels approached his car, he heard the school alarm beeping. He quickly hollered across the parking lot to Mr. Waters who was still at the dumpster. "You need to turn off the school alarm!" Mr. Waters didn't seem to hear him yelling. He yelled a little louder. "School alarm is beeping! Mr. Waters, turn off the school alarm!"

Chapter 17
New Bedtime Stories

"Honey, wake up! Why are you screaming, and who is Mr. Waters?" asked Susan Daniels-Robbins as she reached up and turned off the alarm clock. It was seven-thirty in the morning and Matthew's first day of school.

Dr. Robbins opened his eyes and yawned.

He looked at his wife. "I had the strangest dream. I dreamed about Aaron, your Dad. You know how he's always telling us stories about his boyhood days with all his buddies. Well, I dreamed about him and all his buddies. Part of it was sad, another part was crazy, but most of it was just plain funny, and it all seemed so real."

Susan smiled as she got out of bed. She dressed and went downstairs to fix breakfast. Matthew woke up when he smelled breakfast cooking and joined his Mother in the kitchen.

To celebrate Matthew's first day of school, Susan had bought him a surprise and put it in the den. She showed him his gift and told him he could have it when he finished breakfast. He liked his Mother's surprises. When they returned to the kitchen, Dr. Robbins joined them.

Matthew sat at the table and watched his Mother pour some orange juice while his Dad sat and read the morning newspaper. When Susan sat down to join them, Dr. Robbins saw something that caught his attention. "Would you look at that? The local department store is advertising books about numbers, the alphabet, and phonics."

Susan looked at her husband oddly. "What's so unusual about that? Honey, it *is* the first day of school."

Dr. Robbins laughed. "Oh, it's nothing unusual," he said as he continued reading.

Matthew finished his breakfast and asked to be excused. He headed to the den to see his new things. Before Dr. Robbins finished his breakfast, he heard a voice coming from the den. "Hello, I'm Lavender." *Now, that is unusual,* he thought to himself.

Dr. Robbins quickly stood up and dropped his paper in the floor. He looked at Susan in surprise, "Where is that voice coming from? There was a little book in my dream called *I'm Lavender!*"

Laughing, Susan responded, "Well, I know why you dreamed about that little book, because a lady stopped by this morning really early and got me out of bed. She was selling a whole series of books for children. She came in and talked forever it seemed. I figured the only way to get rid of her was to buy some books. So, I bought a few and went back to bed. You must have heard us talking and dreamed about them. I bought books about dinosaurs, phonics, numbers, the alphabet, and the little book you just heard called *I'm Lavender.* It's real cute. You push a button and it says hello and its name. She also explained that it's a revision of an old *I'm Lavender* basic reading series."

"I'm glad you cleared that up. That explains what I dreamed," responded Dr. Robbins.

Matthew heard his parents talking about his new books. He walked in the kitchen to be with them. "Look Dad, we have new bedtime stories to read tonight," he said as he showed his new books to his Dad.

Right then there was a knock on the front door. Susan hurried to the door and found a note taped on the outside. She read the note as she walked back to the kitchen.

"Hey, you're not going to believe this! They're going to reopen the New England Book Factory across the street."

"They are!!!" answered Dr. Robbins with a wild look in his eyes.

Epilogue

I'm Lavender
My First Reader

When I saw that flash of purple
I knew you at a glance,
After all the years that came and went
We meet again by chance.

Because you were the first one
To come and be with me,
You showed me how important
A friend like you can be.

Now I've seen so many others
Since that first day I was with you,
Some funny, sad, serious and only one true
But none quite as cute as the little one like you.

You taught me much and made me laugh
And gave me simple pleasure,
So now I'm going to take you home
And treasure you forever.

Printed in the United States
32093LVS00006B/334-441